SO MANY SECRETS

BREAKDOWN

VICKI HINZE

MAGNOLIA LEAF PRESS

Copyright © 2018 Vicki Hinze

ISBN: 978-1-939016-19-5

Cover Design by Vicki Hinze

MAGNOLIA LEAF PRESS

Magnolia Leaf Press, Niceville, Florida

First Edition October 2018

so many secrets

A Novel

Chapter 1

Monday, October 8

FIVE DAYS.

Impossible to believe but that's all it had taken for the idyllic vision of Shutter Lake, California, lauded by *Country Living* as the most perfect town in all of America, to prove perfection is a façade and all the safety and security sought and found in it had been an illusion.

One murder. Illusion shattered.

One murder, and so many secrets...

A shiver crept up Dr. Dana Perkins's backbone. She stiffened against it, determined to reclaim her sense of security here. At the deli counter inside Stacked, a block off downtown's main square, she ordered a grilled chicken sandwich with a side salad and a bottle of Evian berry-flavored water, then glanced over to the cluster of two-dozen tables. About half-full. A lot of people were having a late lunch today.

Dana took a table surrounded by empties then settled in and reached for a sheaf of papers from her tote. She had been through the school records at least a dozen times, but maybe in the sandwich shop, she would be more objective, gain some new insight, and see something she had missed.

Oh, but she needed to be certain she hadn't missed anything. After Phoenix, to retain her sanity she had to be absolutely certain she hadn't missed any warning sign.

There had to be a reason this year's best and brightest student had confessed to murder. Some logical, rational reason that Vinn Bradshaw, gifted future nanotechnologist, studious, popular basketball player, who exhibited nothing short of fantastic leadership skills, confessed. Vinn could not have killed anyone much less a prominent Shutter Lake founder's daughter like Sylvia Cole.

Nolan Ikard, about thirty, tall and lean with sandy blond hair and a handsome man's confident swagger, paused at her table. Nolan owned The Grind, a coffee shop sharing a common wall with Stacked that Dana frequented every morning on her walk from home to the school.

"How's our favorite principal?" Nolan asked. "Things settling down any at S.L.S.?"

Many students, current and former, referred to Shutter Lake School as S.L.S. "Getting better," she said because it was expected and not because it was true. "The students are still rattled, but then aren't we all?"

He nodded and avoided her eyes, his own gold-flecked ones clouded and troubled. "Guess the kids won't settle down until their parents do. Maybe we will all get back to normal soon."

"Maybe we will." Dana smiled.

He walked on to his favorite table beside hers and next to the front window. How many times in the last year had she seen him staring out that window as if he had lost his last friend? She'd been tempted often to ask if he was okay, or to offer to listen if he needed to talk, but something had held her back. She couldn't say what, but she always followed her instinctive urges on things like that. In his case, she hoped she didn't live to regret it.

A waitress Dana didn't recognize delivered her order. She must be from Grass Valley. She hadn't been one of Dana's students.

That was a perk of being principal of a school with three-hundred students. You knew them, and they knew you. The other items on the waitress's tray were Nolan's. Cuban sandwich and a side of slaw. A hint of citrus, garlic and a splash of white wine gave the mustard on his sandwich a distinct scent that set her mouth to watering. It smelled spicy and tart, interesting. It smelled great.

When the waitress placed his food on the small square table in front of him, Nolan barely glanced at her. That piqued Dana's curiosity and fired a red-flag warning too bold to ignore. Nolan Ikard not flirting with an eligible woman? Normally, he'd flirt with a lamppost. Oh, not offensive flirting, just friendly flirting. It was as natural to him as breathing. But not today.

Apparently his perfect façade of Shutter Lake also had shattered —and Dana certainly shouldn't make too much of it. Everyone in the community seemed disturbed and wary and disillusioned these days.

Shifting her thoughts to her work, she studied the details in Vinn's files and nibbled at her food, wishing she'd dared to order Nolan's hot and spicy Cuban. Stacked made the best sandwiches and slaw in the tri-county area, but with Dana's stomach acting up since Vinn's confession, she didn't dare to risk eating anything not mild.

About a third of the way through the teachers' observation notes, she spotted Kristina Sharapova's name. Her image sprang to mind: long dark hair and eyes, pale skin and a mischievous smile that was nothing short of infectious because it was so rare. Kristina bent toward being serious, which was normal for a teenage Russian exchange student. They competed so fiercely for the chance to come to Shutter Lake to study.

Thanks to the wealthy and childless benefactors, the Windermeres, there were always foreign exchange students at Shutter Lake School. Attending there was an amazing opportunity for all the students really. A group of the most gifted professionals in the world in science, medicine, and industry designed and created the nearly self-sustaining community and they often shared their vast pool of knowledge and expertise with the students.

Dana was proud of the program she and Mayor Thomas Jessup had created. In two short years, its success rate at preparing knowledgeable, socially mature and motivated graduates had surpassed expectations and her wildest dreams.

On Kristina's first day with them, she had been like a fish out of water. Who wouldn't be? Strange school, no familiar friends or faces. Living in a strange country and speaking a foreign language. But Vinn Bradshaw had picked up on her uneasiness. Without prompting, he'd taken her under his wing and helped her fit in. They were, according to the file observation note, good friends.

Dana too had been wrong about that. She reached into her tote for a pen, accidentally pulled out a large Ziploc bag, and smiled to herself. Every teacher she'd ever known carried a waterproof bag in her handbag or tote. Old habits die hard. Stuffing the frosted bag back in, she snagged the pen and then scribbled a new note on a page she had labeled "Things to tell Laney."

Laney Holt was the Deputy Chief of Police and lead investigator on Sylvia Cole's murder case. A beautiful young blond who favored long hair and ponytails over short red hair like Dana's and, guessing, a year or two younger than Dana's thirty-four. *Not just friends.* She added the note to the list.

Laney Holt breezed by Dana's table with an order of fries and a bottle of flavored water then dropped into a seat at Nolan's table.

He didn't look happy to see her.

Gauging by the level look she laid on him, she wasn't happy to see him either. "I still need your DNA," Laney told Nolan.

Dana didn't deliberately listen but, when people seated three feet from you talk, unless you cotton-stuff your ears, you can't help overhearing their conversation.

"Why?" Surprise flickered through Nolan's eyes. "You've got your killer. Word's out all over the lake Vinn Bradshaw confessed."

Laney finished chewing a fry, swallowed and then sipped from her water bottle. "Paperwork," she said.

"You want my blood to check off a box to make sure your case sticks?" He shot her a resent-laced look of disgust.

"Exactly." Her lips curved in a smile that never touched her eyes.

"And?" He pushed.

"And a witness saw a man fitting your description running away from Sylvia Cole's house the night she was murdered. Chief McCabe wants no loose ends."

"I don't care what McCabe wants." Nolan frowned. "You clowns get a description that fits half the men around here and naturally you come after me."

Laney's voice stiffened, but her expression appeared as calm as it had before the tension between them rocketed. "This *clown* is trying to eliminate you as a possibility, Ikard." She tilted her head. "Wait a second. Are you saying it was you?"

Silence.

Laney bit into another fry, let the silence stretch, yawn, settle. Finally, she asked, "Did Sylvia tell you she was planning a vacation to Venezuela?"

Dana's heart rate sped. She kept her nose down and her gaze focused on her papers. One night after Yoga class at the Community Gathering Center, Sylvia had told Dana about that trip. A few weeks ago, Sylvia had even come to Dana's cottage to see her mask collection. They'd talked for a few hours. Before Phoenix and coming to Shutter Lake, Dana had loved to travel. She'd spent her summers exploring, including three trips to Venezuela.

Nolan answered Laney. "Sylvia didn't tell me anything about any vacation anywhere. We didn't talk much."

"So was it you—running away from her house that night?"

"No."

As if she hadn't heard him, Laney went on. "There's one thing I don't understand." She polished off her last fry, took a long draw on her water. "Why did you climb out of the window instead of leaving through the door?"

No answer.

She dusted the salt from her fingertips with a paper napkin. "I get that Shutter Lake is a small community and maybe you two didn't want to broadcast your intimate relationship, but…the window?"

"I told you." Nolan's jaw tightened and he leaned forward in his seat. "Sylvia and I were friends back in school. It was a long time ago. You knew her. That woman had no interest in a relationship with me or anyone else. She was as independent as people come."

"Just in it for the sex. Got it." Not one to cower, Laney leaned in, spoke to him nearly nose to nose. "So you went out the window to show her you're independent, too. Uh-huh. Well, that makes perfect sense." Her sarcasm couldn't be missed. She scooted back her seat then stood up. "You've got twenty-four hours to come to the station and handle that DNA sample."

"Or what?" he said, his voice a sharp and cutting tone Dana had never before heard him utter. "No. You know what? Forget it." He glared up at Laney. "You want my DNA, get with my lawyer."

"You have a lawyer?" Laney bared her teeth in a would-be smile. "Does he have a name?"

"Morris Barton."

Her smile turned genuine. "Ah, here's a tip. You might want to start looking for a replacement. Barton is Vinn's lawyer." She turned. "Twenty-four hours, Ikard."

Nolan didn't draw a breath until Laney exited the door of Stacked and stepped out onto the sidewalk.

Muttering and agitated, he finished his meal.

Dana ordered a cup of coffee, studied her papers with her mind whirling, and waited.

Finally, Nolan left and, when the door closed behind him, she phoned Laney. "You need to come back to Stacked right away."

"What's wrong?"

"Nothing. Just get back here as fast as you can." Dana caught the waitress two steps away from Nolan's table. "Don't touch anything."

The startled waitress jerked back and darted a worried look at Dana. "What?"

"Don't touch anything on that table." Dana hated this. But

Vinn's whole future could ride on what happened next, and no one was going to rob him of it. Not on her watch.

Scant minutes later, Laney entered Stacked and rushed straight over to Dana. "What's wrong?"

"I told you on the phone, nothing is wrong."

Laney stilled, parked a hand on her hip. "Then why am I here, Dana?"

"On TV, I saw an investigator going through a person of interest's trash. The can wasn't on his property, it was at the curb, waiting for the collector. He said once trash is abandoned, it's legal for him to look in it for evidence. Is that true?"

"Well, yes," Laney said, looking a little bewildered. "If it can be proven that it wasn't contaminated."

Dana rubbed an itch at her earlobe, tugging it. "Meaning, no one else touched the abandoned trash?"

"Right."

Dana nodded toward Nolan's table. "Well, Nolan Ikard abandoned his trash at that table and left Stacked. His DNA is on that fork and glass."

Laney's eyes narrowed. "Has anyone—"

Dana cut in. "The waitress delivered his food, but since he abandoned the trash, the table and departed, no one else has come near that table. It's untouched," Dana said. "I'll swear to it."

Laney nodded, appreciation lighting her eyes. "Let me grab an evidence bag."

Dana pulled the Ziploc from her purse. "Here you go."

A smile curled Laney's lips. "How long has that puppy been in your purse?"

Good question. One Dana couldn't answer. "Not a clue."

"Best use mine, then." Laney retrieved a bag and gathered the evidence. She turned to the waitress. "You can clear the table now. Thanks for waiting."

Dana gathered her papers and put them back into the sheath, then dumped the file into her tote.

Laney stepped over to her, the filled evidence bag in hand. "Thanks."

"You're welcome."

"Why did you do this?" Laney's sunglasses rested parked atop her head.

"I couldn't help but overhear your conversation. An opportunity arose, so…"

"You seized it. I see." Laney faced Dana squarely. "You're convinced Vinn is innocent."

"I know he is innocent, Laney. Just as I know, until the real murderer is behind bars, I have three hundred other kids still in jeopardy."

"How do you know Vinn's confession isn't real? You're a school principal and a psychologist, for heaven's sake. You know better than most that given the right circumstances anyone can kill."

"Yes, of course, I do. But Vinn didn't. For those same reasons, I know that, too," Dana said quietly. "I just can't prove it."

"I hear an unspoken *yet* on the end of that remark." Compassion crossed Laney's face and settled into a frown. "Dana, you want to protect your students. I get that. I want to protect them, too."

"Of course, you do."

"Well, then. Let's do what we do best. You are the pro at the school, so I won't try to run it, and I'm the pro at police work, so don't you try to run my investigation, okay? Just do your job and let me do my job."

"Sharing a few notes, but I wouldn't dream of interfering."

Laney cleared her throat. "Course not." She backed up a step and checked her watch. "If I hurry, I can get this to the lab before the press conference."

"Don't forget girls' night out. Wednesday night."

"Seven o'clock. The Wine and Cheese House," Laney said. "I'll be there." She stopped and looked back. "Did you remind Julia?"

"She's on my list," Dana said. Julia Ford, a former investigative journalist who now wrote a weekly column for *The Firefly*, their community newspaper, which also ran in *The Sacramento Bee*, tended to forget. Actually, trying to forget is what had brought her to Shutter Lake—not that anyone knew it, and those who did, like Dana, were sworn to secrecy on the subject. "I told Ana, too," Dana added. Dr. Ana Perez ran the medical clinic. She was single like the rest of them and she might be able to offer valuable insight on Vinn.

"Sounds good," Laney said, then rushed out the door on her way to the lab.

Dana gathered the rest of her things. With luck, she could catch Thomas at his office. If anyone could get Chief McCabe to let her in to see Vinn, it'd be the mayor. One way or another, she had to get in to see Vinn.

If Thomas Jessup'd had half as much trouble calming the community as she'd had calming her staff, students and their parents, they both could use a soothing word, a quiet dinner and a stiff drink. Maybe two...

Chapter 2

Dana left Stacked and walked east. Passing The Grind, the rich, robust smell of coffee filled the air. Though tempted to slip in and grab a Macchiato Espresso, she remembered her delicate stomach and kept walking through the square's park, taking the cobblestone trail to the center fountain, then continued on to the street and crossed to the sidewalk. Normally, she would have lingered on one of the many benches and watched the toddlers play or the old men engaged in their games of chess, but she lacked the time to indulge in that luxury today. City Hall occupied most of the block, but she veered left to the mayor's office next door, and then stepped inside.

"Dr. Perkins, hello," Thomas Jessup's new silver-haired receptionist said.

"Hi, Gracie." Dana nodded, hoping she'd recalled the woman's name correctly. "I need five minutes. Is he in?"

"Just a moment." She dropped her voice to a whisper. "Let me clear his office."

"Thank you."

Gracie, a woman in her late fifties with intelligent eyes she hid behind wide-framed dark-tinted glasses, was a new edition to Shutter Lake and to the mayor's office. There had been a little scuttlebutt that his former assistant, the young and elegant head-turner Alyssa, had committed the ultimate sin of falling in love with her boss. Thomas had fired her on the spot and hired Gracie as her replacement. The hushed gossip ended on a dime.

Everyone in the lake knew two things about Mayor Thomas Jessup: At thirty-six, he was a vibrant, handsome clotheshorse who projected the polished, sophisticated look and tone the founders sought, and Thomas was a perfectionist when it came to appearances and images—for Shutter Lake and himself. He wasn't interested in long-term commitments or relationships that made demands, and he wanted absolutely no part of love.

Why? Dana wasn't sure, though it made for a great relationship between them. They worked well together and often brainstormed projects and ideas beneficial to the community. They were friends, trusted confidants and sounding boards for each other, but things never got personal to the point of being uncomfortable or complicated. Even seven years after Phoenix, she wasn't ready for demands or complications and, if she had to guess, Thomas Jessup would never be ready for them.

Gracie reappeared and waved. "You can go in now, Dr. Perkins."

"Thank you." Dana walked down the short hallway, her short stacked heels clicking on the wooden floor, to the double doors that stood open, leading to the mayor's inner sanctum. Before she entered, the comforting scents of of lemon polish and old money reached out to greet her.

"Dana." Thomas stood behind an enormous desk, intricately carved in rich mahogany. While the reception area was thoroughly modern, Thomas's preferred style as well as Dana's own, the mayor's office was detailed traditional. Official, rich in history and the tasteful swagger of understated success. The effect was reassuring, stable and secure.

"Sorry to barge in on you, Thomas." Dana moved to the visitor's chair near his desk. "Didn't you have on a gray suit this morning?"

"I did." His green eyes twinkled. "But black works best for the press conference."

"Ah, of course." It did add a special sparkle to his green eyes. "Five o'clock, right?"

He sat down. "Yes." His smile faded. "You'll be able to make it —in case there are questions about the school or students?"

She hadn't planned on it, but his point was valid. "I'll be there."

He rewarded her with a dazzling smile. "So is this just a friendly visit, or what can I do for you?"

Straight and to the point. One of his best assets. "A bit of both. I asked Chief McCabe for permission to see Vinn."

"Okay." Thomas sat back in his large executive chair, giving her his full attention.

"He said no."

"Did he say why?" Fidgeting with his pen, Thomas thumbed it on his leather blotter.

"Not really. He just refused."

"So...?"

Thomas was going to make her ask. He knew she hated asking anyone for anything, but for Vinn... "So I want you to talk to him and see if you can change his mind."

"I'm sorry, but I can't do that." Regret crossed Thomas's face. "You know I don't interfere in McCabe's investigations."

"Technically, it's Laney's investigation. He put her in charge because she has homicide experience—from her detective days in Los Angeles."

"I'm aware of Laney Holt's previous employment, Dana. But I can't interfere with her investigations either. It's a sign to residents and the press that won't be missed."

"What sign?"

"That I don't trust either of them to do their jobs." He lifted a shoulder. "It's the same sign you don't want—the council interfering, implying you can't run your school."

"But this is more important than perceptions, Thomas. This is about Vinn's life."

"Your school is about all the students' lives, and McCabe's investigations are about all our lives. Those are equally important, you surely agree." Regret flashed through Thomas's eyes, softened his tone. "I do wish I could help you."

"We always help each other."

"I know we do, which makes it difficult to refuse you anything. But this time, on this request, I have no choice. I can't do it." He paused a second. "Look, I understand how Sylvia's murder has impacted our community. It has been hard on all of us, especially on those of us in public service. But Vinn confessing... It's been particularly difficult for you. I get that, Dana. Vinn is gifted. No doubt about it. You've invested in him, and you had such high hopes for his future."

She resented the unspoken reminder of what had happened in Phoenix. His assumption that some misplaced sense of guilt drove her on this with Vinn. She'd be in this chair no matter which of her students sat in that jail cell. "I invest in all my students, Thomas, and one of them has confessed to a murder I don't believe he's capable of committing, much less that he did commit. But I also have two-hundred ninety-nine more students in potential jeopardy. I need to find out what really happened, for all their sakes."

"As do I, which is why our highly qualified police department and county forensics team have access to any experts they might need. The best law enforcement minds in the business are all available to them."

The council had approved throwing whatever money was necessary to finding the killer. Great news. Fabulous news. So far, all that hadn't done a thing to help Vinn. "I want to talk with him, Thomas."

His tone chilled to ice. "I will not counter McCabe's orders."

"You can—"

"I won't." Thomas relaxed his tense jaw. "Have you even discussed visiting Vinn with his parents?"

"Of course, I have." She nodded. "Connie called me the day after Vinn confessed. She was desolate."

"So you put on your psychologist hat and talked her off the ledge."

"I tried to help her cope with extremely upsetting news. You know how close she and Vinn are."

An emotion Dana couldn't tag swam across Thomas's face. He quickly masked it. "He's a mama's boy, and I'm sure Connie is devastated." Thomas laced his fingers atop his desk, squeezed until his knuckles went white. "What parent wouldn't be?"

"I'd say her reaction is pretty universal to mothers in this unenviable situation," Dana admitted, trying to peg Thomas's odd undertone. He wasn't a parent, but he seemed to be identifying as one. Maybe that identification was a skill he'd acquired in his position. Being mayor would require the ability to relate to all residents, and many of them were parents. "Anyway, Connie gave me permission to see Vinn, but McCabe won't honor it."

"And he didn't say why?"

"No, he didn't," Dana said. "Frankly, he didn't seem much in the mood for conversation." She didn't mention the faint whiff of alcohol she'd sensed. There had been no evidence of it in his speech, and she hadn't been able to see his eyes. Sunglasses. Probably just mouthwash. She'd told herself that then, and reminded herself of it now.

Thomas swiped at his cuff, avoiding her eyes. "When did you speak to him?"

"On my way to school. First thing in the morning."

Thomas's expression lightened. "There's your problem."

"My problem?" Bewildered, Dana hiked her shoulders.

"Here's a secret to put in your back pocket—but it'll cost you."

Invoking the game often played between them. That had to be a good sign. "Terms?"

"Dinner. Tonight at your house. And you make that Mongolian beef dish of yours."

Thomas did love her Mongolian. "Deal—no bribery, just a friendly dinner between colleagues."

"No bribery." He smiled his agreement.

"So what's this non-bribe secret I just didn't buy?"

"McCabe is a night owl. He's cranky in the morning. Anything

14

you want him to refuse, you ask early in the morning. If you want him to agree, ask him in the late afternoon. The later, the better."

Dana laughed. "Now that would have been handy information to have before I asked him the first time, Thomas. Why didn't you share that insightful tidbit before?"

"If I had, you wouldn't be here and I wouldn't be coming to dinner tonight."

"You're incorrigible. Shameless, too."

"Definitely."

"So you'll speak to him?"

"No, I'm afraid I still can't do that." Thomas sat back, dragged his teeth over his lower lip. "But you might ask him again tomorrow. You never know. He could change his mind."

"Late in the day."

"Definitely."

"I appreciate the advice, and at the moment he might be experiencing at least a little good will in my direction."

"How so?"

She told him about Nolan Ikard and the DNA event at Stacked.

"Well done, Dana, and. . .interesting." Thomas dipped his square chin, and a wicked glint lit in his eye. "Guess you're going to have to back off the kids about watching so much TV."

"You're merciless, Thomas Jessup." Dana stood up. "Seven o'clock," she said. "And bring wine."

"Wait." He grabbed the edge of his desk. "Don't go. I want to talk to you about something."

Dana stopped. "What is it?"

He turned serious. Walked from the desk to the wall of shelves filled with awards and honors. "I'm not sure how to approach this." He studied the plaques as if seeing them for the first time.

"What is it, Thomas?" She moved to his side. "Just say it."

He searched her face. "You're a good person, Dana."

Her heart fluttered. "Are you going beta on me, or what?" It was a commonly shared joke between them. Acting out of character, overly emotional, strange for them.

"No," he said, then paused. "Maybe." Another pause. "Well, in a way, yeah, I guess I am."

She didn't bother to hide her surprise. "On what?"

He shook his head. "You know what, let's leave it for now. We've got the press conference and I need to get my head into it. We'll talk about my beta moment tonight after dinner—if that's okay with you?" He swiped at his broad forehead. "I do want to talk to you about something, but I was wrong. This isn't the right time."

"Okay." She had no idea what to make of that, but at least she wouldn't have to wonder what was at the heart of it for too long. A couple hours, and he'd be ready to share this…whatever his beta moment was. "Thomas, are you afraid the murderer is still out there and something else will happen?" She took a guess based on her own fears.

"I can't say that hasn't crossed my mind." Thomas let out a deep breath that hiked his shoulders. "But that's not what this is about."

"Okay." She backed up a step, giving him a little more space so he didn't feel crowded. "Whenever you're ready."

"Don't dread it, Dana. It's nothing to do with you or Shutter Lake. It's about me."

That concerned her even more. If Thomas Jessup was getting personal, it had to be something significant. "You're not ill." She said it and prayed it was true.

"No. It's nothing like that." He smiled and a tenderness she never had seen in him filled his eyes. "But it's nice to know you'd be that concerned if I were."

"I don't have so many friends that I can squander one, Thomas. Especially not one I can confide in without filters."

That was true, and something they'd discussed on several occasions. Even in non-work related interactions, he could never forget he was the mayor, and she could never forget she was the school principal people were trusting with their kids. They weren't allowed the public flaws and insecurities, challenges or shortcomings that all people have. It was their job to, at all times, project control and calm and competence.

And since Sylvia Cole's murder and Vinn Bradshaw's arrest, that had been a hard road to walk in Shutter Lake.

Gracie appeared in the open doorway. "Sorry to interrupt, Mayor Jessup."

"What is it, Gracie?" he asked.

"Vernon Bradshaw needs a minute."

As Gracie spoke, Vernon Bradshaw brushed past her shoulder and entered the office. A bold move that clearly surprised Gracie as much as it did Thomas and Dana.

"I want my son out of jail, Jessup," Vernon said.

The billionaire pharmaceutical company owner strode across the wooden floor to face Thomas. "Put him on an ankle monitor or something, but let him come home." He dragged an unsteady hand through his dark hair. The gray at his temples winked in the light. "Connie hasn't stopped crying since this all started."

At the mention of Connie, Thomas's expression softened, filled with compassion. "I know this is hard on your family but I can't release Vinn, Vernon. He's confessed to murder."

"I know what he said, but you don't understand. Connie is losing it. I can't watch my wife falling apart like this and do nothing." He lifted a hand toward Dana. "Did you go see him? Connie said you were going to go see him. But earlier today, he said you hadn't been there."

"Not yet." Dana didn't mention McCabe's denying her permission. Vernon would just erupt on him next, so she kept it to herself. "The students have needed my attention at school, as I'm sure you understand. They're unaccustomed to dealing with a tragedy of this nature."

"So are we." He darted his gaze from Dana to Thomas and back again. "Why can't Vinn come home? People are placed on house arrest all the time."

"Not for violent crimes," Thomas said.

"Violent? You know Vinn. He doesn't have a violent bone in his body."

"Vernon, he confessed to strangling a woman to death," Thomas stated baldly. "That's violent."

Vernon clamped his jaw shut, swung his gaze to Dana. "Go see him, Dr. Perkins. Make it a priority. I don't know what the hell has gotten into his head, but you figure it out. I can't lose my son and my wife. This whole thing has Connie teetering on the edge." He pivoted to Thomas. "She jumps or even falls over it, and I'm not going to be a happy man, Jessup."

Acknowledging his understanding, Thomas nodded. "None of us will be happy, Vernon."

A truer statement, Dana thought, had never been spoken. If Vernon Bradshaw wasn't happy, he would make it his personal mission in life to make sure no one in Shutter Lake was happy. Unfortunately, he had the power and money to liberally spread misery. Lots and lots of misery...

Chapter 3

A cluster of people stood gathered outside City Hall, which housed the police station. A podium stood empty with media microphones attached. The major networks, cable news, Grass Valley's local network, and print reporters from *The Sacramento Bee* and even a *New York Times* reporter Dana recognized huddled together, surrounded by residents.

Spotting Julia and Ana, Dana joined them. "Surprised to see you two here."

"Afternoon walk," Julia said. "Ana needed a break from the clinic."

"Reminder. Girls' night out—"

"Wednesday at seven, The Wine and Cheese House. Got your text." Julia scanned the crowd.

"I'll be there, barring any emergency." Ana leaned forward to see Dana around Julia.

Showing up was at best fifty-fifty odds with Dr. Ana Perez, which Dana guessed was about par for a doctor running a top-notch clinic with all the latest equipment money could buy. Smart, rich seniors who remained icons in their respective fields, demanded excellent everything in health care for themselves and their families. Ana did her best to provide it.

Julia's blond hair caught the sunlight slanting in through the trees. The woman had beautiful skin and an even more beautiful mind. Her former work as an investigative journalist in some of the most brutal and ravaged places in the world would have scarred most, but somehow she had managed to find balance. "All is well with my soul," she'd whisper when she needed to center herself.

That ability to center had thus far escaped Dana. Oh, there was a time when she was peaceful, but Phoenix had ended that. There's just no coming back from that kind of thing. It changes everything. Alters your entire life. Yes, you get better at coping with it, but peace? Peace becomes a faded, distant memory. If she lost Vinn, it'd be a haunting memory, too. She shivered.

"Well now," Julia whispered to Dana and Ana. "That's interesting."

"What?" Dana followed Julia's line of vision to Thomas Jessup. "He changed suits. Gray to black. It's better for press conferences."

Julia rolled her gaze. "I wasn't looking at his clothes, Dana."

Dana took a second look. Thomas stood near Connie and Vernon Bradshaw. They weren't speaking, just standing there. Connie seemed to have aged overnight and Vernon's face had become a mask that hid every emotion known to man.

"Some things expensive clothes and hair-stylists can't fix." Julia dragged in air from between her teeth.

"No, they can't," Ana said. "I've never seen Connie look that… maxed out."

"She couldn't care less about her appearance right now," Dana said. "Her son's life is on the line."

"I wasn't talking about her." Julia turned to look at Dana. "I was talking about him."

"Vernon?"

"Jessup." Julia grunted. "Dana, sometimes you blow me away. Can't you see how worried he looks?"

"Of course, he's worried. We're all worried."

Julia and Ana shared a look. "Not that kind of worried."

Impatient, Dana lifted a hand. "What are you talking about?"

"Seriously?"

"Yes, seriously."

"Dana," Julia whispered. "Haven't you ever noticed how much Vinn favors Mayor Jessup?"

Whatever Dana might have expected Julia to say, that wasn't it. It sank in. She thought of Vinn and really looked at Thomas.

"She never noticed," Julia told Ana.

Ana ignored her.

No sense trying to hide it. Dana hadn't ever noticed. "I never thought about it."

Julia prodded Ana. "You ever notice?"

"Oh, no." Ana lifted a rebellious hand. "You're not dragging me into this. I never discuss patients."

With a little shake of her head, Julia warned Dana. "You might want to check that out. Look at the bone structure." Julia adjusted her sunglasses. "Jessup's a clotheshorse, we all know that, and Vinn is… well, not, shall we say. But the bones don't lie."

Dana frowned at Julia, who shrugged. "Just saying."

Swiveling her gaze back to Thomas, Dana looked at him as if for the first time, and the similarities between him and Vinn smacked her hard. The bone structure told the truth. Dana frowned and puzzled through the situation. Connie was nearly twenty years older than Thomas, for pity's sake. Despite the similarities, Julia had to be out of her mind on this one.

But was she? Connie had been a teacher at the school when Thomas had been a student there. Good grief, it was impossible. Absurd even thinking about such an implication.

"It's not impossible, is it?" Julia whispered.

Dana opened her mouth to deny it, but couldn't seem to utter a sound. It wasn't impossible. She surely wouldn't be the first teacher to have an affair with a male student. But, oh, Dana hated to think she had for both their sakes and especially for Vinn's.

"Sometimes it's hard to see things when they're hiding in plain sight, right under your nose."

Dana searched for the words to refute Julia, but the truth was

Thomas had reacted oddly in his office to Vernon, and Vinn did strongly favor Thomas. How had she not noticed that before now?

Fortunately, McCabe had taken to the podium and was addressing the crowd. Camera shutters clicked and flashed, and cameramen held their equipment on their shoulders, recording the event. Dana heard very little of it. Her mind swam from Thomas to Vinn, to Connie and Vernon, then back to Thomas. Was Vinn the cause of Thomas's beta moment?

"Get real, McCabe." Heidi Udall shouted out. Short and heavy-set, she wore her Batter Up Bakery uniform of a white shirt and black-and-white checked skirt and hat. "That scrawny kid couldn't have strangled Sylvia Cole to death. In hand-to-hand, Sylvia could take him."

Gasps silenced the crowd.

Heidi's jaw dropped open. "Did I say that out loud?" Clearly horrified, she looked at the faces of those around her which confirmed that she hadn't just spoken it, she'd shouted it. "I'm so—"

"Unbearable, Heidi Udall." Connie Bradshaw glared at her. "That scrawny kid is my son. My son who had dreams of being a brilliant nanotechnologist to perfect better drug delivery systems for people like you—all of you. He was a basketball player, a friend to many of your children. He had a life. All of it is gone now. Everything is… gone."

Vernon moved to circle an arm around her. She shoved him away. "No. Don't you touch me. I will have my say, Vernon."

He held up his hands and backed up a step. "You were right about one thing, Heidi. Vinn didn't kill anyone, and only a fool would believe he did."

"He confessed, didn't he?" A man shouted from the back of the crowd.

"He didn't do it." Connie got a wild look in her eyes. "I'm going to get him, and I'm taking him home. Right now." She powered through the crowd.

"This is going to get nasty," Julia warned.

"Very." Dana motioned toward the doors. "Come on."

Connie pushed her way into City Hall. Dana, Julia and Ana

blocked the entry from the top of the steps. A cameraman did his best to push through to get inside.

"Not a good time," Dana said, holding her ground.

Julia wasn't as subtle. "One more step and it's assault, Jack. Back up or face-plant the steps. Your call."

The crowd turned its attention from the podium to the doors behind Dana and the women. Jessup and McCabe made their way up the steps. Dana and Julia parted so they could pass and go inside.

"Thanks," Thomas said.

When the door opened behind them, Connie's screams could be heard. Her arguing with Laney, who was sympathetic but insistent that Connie couldn't take Vinn anywhere. Thomas's voice blended into the mix.

The crowd waited silently, fixated on the door and straining to hear what was being said inside. Long minutes passed, tension ratcheted up. But it was Laney Holt who appeared in the cracked open doorway, not Connie Bradshaw. "Dr. Perez," Laney said. "We could use a little help here."

The screaming continued for long, tense minutes. The pharmacist from across the street rushed up the steps, carrying a small white prescription bag. "Dr. Ana—"

Dana and Julia parted and let him pass.

"She's lost it," Julia said. "Ana's going to knock her on her—"

"She's terrified." Dana smiled reassuringly at the crowd. "If this were you, and he was your child, wouldn't you be terrified?"

Thomas's voice was soft and soothing at her back. "Connie, this isn't the way. Let Ana help you. We're going to get to the bottom of all this. I promise you, we will."

"I don't believe you," Connie spat. "You have his confession. Why would you even look for anyone else?"

"We are looking at everyone else," McCabe assured her.

"That's right," Thomas said. "What we need is for you to get a grip and let us do what we need to do to find out the truth, Connie. We all want the truth. You keep Chief McCabe and Deputy Chief Holt tied up with you, that's time they're not—"

"But this is my son, Thomas." Her voice cracked and broke and the screaming started all over again.

"Ana," McCabe said. "Do it."

"I can't. She's in no condition to authorize—"

"Dana," Thomas shouted to be heard above Connie's screams. "Get Vernon."

More spectators had joined the crowd, and a torrent of intense speculation was going on. Dana cringed. Vernon stood in the center of the group watching everyone, his mask in place. "Vernon," she called to him and then motioned him to her. "Dr. Perez needs you inside."

He went in and shut the doors behind him.

A few minutes later, the sobs so deep they tore at the soul ceased. Dana caught her first calming breath. "Okay, everyone. Let's break this up now. And please, when you talk about this in front of the children, remember that they're looking to you to see how they should react. If you're calm, they'll be calm. We've had more than enough upset, right? So be calm."

People began milling away and soon the crowd had dispersed. "I can't believe Heidi Udall said that."

"Neither can she," Dana told Julia. The last of the lingerers and gawkers abandoned the area, though tongues would wag about what had happened here for weeks. Maybe longer.

"True." Julia dipped her sunglasses low on her nose, looked at Dana over the top of them. "I can't believe all this." Her resentment shone through as clear as the streaks of sun on the sidewalk. "I came here to get away from this kind of thing."

Dana sighed her empathy. "Didn't we all?"

Chapter 4

Dana's cottage on Mill Street had character.

White clapboard trimmed in black with an inviting wide front porch, it charmed her. It had the first moment she had seen it, and it did now, seven years later.

She shifted the packages in her arm, careful to keep the box from Batter Up Bakery from tipping. The individual strawberry cheesecakes didn't handle tips well. She keyed the lock and went inside, cut through the entry to the kitchen, dumped her handbag, keys and tote on the broad granite bar, then put the bakery box into the fridge.

Two hours later, Thomas arrived. He'd changed into a gray suit again. For him, that qualified as casual. Dana smiled.

Rubbing the night chill from his hands, he walked in. "Something smells great."

"That's non-bribe Mongolian Beef."

"That, too," he said, sniffing. "Sweet garlic soy sauce and onions, but something else." He set the bottle of wine on the brown-swirled granite bar. "I can't peg it."

"Wonton soup, my special brown fried rice, and broccoli."

He stilled. "Should I have brought dessert?"

"We're covered." Dana hadn't forgotten Thomas had a sweet tooth. In his book, a meal wasn't a meal without dessert. "Strawberry cheesecake."

"You even made strawberry cheesecake?"

"No way. Why should I bake when Heidi Udall makes the best desserts in town?" Dana retrieved the corkscrew from the top drawer and then passed it to him. "Of course, you have to catch her in the mood, on the right day, to get one of your favorites." Heidi baked what she pleased on any given day. Cupcakes, she baked every day, but her specialty items were strictly potluck for the buyer. She followed her whims and what she baked when was solely her call. You could buy or not until she ran out or closed shop for the day.

"We got lucky. She won't make strawberry cheesecake unless the strawberries are just right."

"Ripe but firm," Dana said. It was a great marketing gimmick. Shoppers dropped in to see what whim she was indulging that day. Most left with something. "And sweet."

"Exactly." He poured the wine into waiting glasses.

Dana checked the wine bottle. "Fetzer Gewürztraminer 2007. I'm not sure I've ever had it."

"It's supposed to be thick and sweet enough for dessert, but the perfect varietal for flash-fried Mongolian Beef. At least, that's what the wine sommelier said."

"What is a wine sommelier?"

"The wine steward at Fitzgerald's," Thomas whispered. "I had no idea what wine went with Mongolian Beef so I called and asked. That's what he recommended."

"Works for me." Fitzgerald's was an upscale restaurant on Shutter Lake. Literally. From the shore, you walk down a wooden dock to it or you arrive by boat. The entire restaurant was built on stilts and surrounded by water. Beautiful sunsets regardless of where you're seated, inside or on the wrap-around deck, and a bit pricy. Dana had been there for special occasions, but never for dinner. Sunday brunch, when Julia, who ate there often, joined her, Laney and Ana. That was the best time for them to plan being off from work.

Thomas often spoke of the beautiful sunsets there, though Dana couldn't imagine they were any more beautiful than sitting in the dirt on the bank of the lake itself. Maybe the glow of the sun shimmering on the water was more magnificent from higher up, but she loved the view from the bank.

In the cottage's dining room, Dana and Thomas enjoyed a pleasant dinner, chatting about light and ordinary things. Though curious about the topic of his beta-moment conversation, she wasn't so curious she wanted to risk the spice in dinner and any added tension. One or the other, she could handle. But since Sylvia's murder had resurrected Dana's Phoenix ghosts, she wasn't brave enough to tackle both simultaneously. Her stomach felt far too fragile. And, honesty forced her to admit, her heart was right there with it.

When they'd finished their meal, she said, "Let's have dessert on the patio." He hadn't yet seen her renovations.

"Okay." He slanted her a questioning look.

She ignored it. So he wasn't enthused, but he had agreed. Not that she blamed him. The last time they'd sat on her patio, it'd been in two lawn chairs on the stone with a TV tray serving as a table between them. The makeover out there had been long, hard work, but the results were lovely. Warm and inviting. She prepared a tray with the individual cheesecakes and a carafe of piping-hot coffee, added cups and saucers, napkins and silverware, and then they headed out the back door.

"Wow! Dana, you've been busy." Thomas looked shocked, and pleased. "I like it."

"Thank you." The stone patio was draped in white netting with bold black stripes at the two outer corners. Huge thick pillows in black-and-white geometric shapes circled a fire-pit and a slice of a tree on a short stump made a great side-table. Atop it burned three white candles. "Have a seat."

They sat near each other and she served the cheesecake and coffee.

"I like this," he said, clearly enjoying the crackling fire and its warmth.

"I do, too." Her smile was genuine and heart-felt. She'd worked for weeks to get the patio and tiered stone beds just the way she wanted them. In spring, she'd enjoy a profusion of colored flowers. It seemed simple now—the design and layout and finishing touches. It sure hadn't been when she was doing it.

"I wouldn't have gone so bold, but I really do like it." He glanced over at her. "It's so you."

"It's great, and that's that, Thomas. Eat your cheesecake."

"All I meant was I love it that you take risks and try things. Bold things." He picked up his fork. "It was a compliment, Dana."

"Oh. Thank you, then." She savored the first bite of strawberry cheesecake. "Oh, why would anyone make this themselves when Heidi is baking?"

"I can't imagine. The woman might say things she shouldn't without realizing it, but give her the due she deserves. She's a fantastic baker."

His reference was to Heidi's shouted scrawny-kid comment to McCabe at the press conference that had set Connie off like a rocket. "Yes, she's a wonder." Dana sipped the hot coffee and watched him through the rising steam. "Have the concerned-citizens calls slowed down at your office?"

He nodded. "Down today, first day." His expression clouded. "But after that gaggle of a press conference this afternoon, I expect tomorrow will be a nightmare. I warned Gracie to bring her Patience."

"I expect she brings her patience to work everyday or she wouldn't be there."

"That, too. But I meant Patience, Gracie's cat." He polished off the cheesecake. "Having her around soothes Gracie and the people coming in seem to like her."

Ambience. "Ah, I see." Dana smiled to herself. It was hard to imagine Thomas Jessup letting a cat run loose in his prim and proper office. But if he thought it was positive imagery, he would tolerate and encourage it. Or maybe Gracie was loosening him up a little.

"What's so funny?"

"Nothing at all. I just, well, I think it's charming that you let Gracie bring her cat to the office."

"It makes her happy. When she's happy, my work goes more smoothly. It's that simple."

"Right." Dana could see the logic in that remark, but Thomas was a softie at heart and even if he didn't know it, Dana did. Apparently, so did Gracie. "I'm holding another 'Express Yourself' assembly for the students tomorrow."

"Again already?"

She nodded. "After the press conference, the parents are bound to go home and get the kids all worked up. Which means we have to calm them down again or we'll lose another day of actually teaching them anything."

Thomas tilted his head, set down his cup on the wide lip of the fire-pit. "I've been meaning to tell you something for a long time, and I just haven't. But now it seems right, if you're up to it…"

"Of course," she said on auto-pilot, then prayed whatever he said wasn't something awful. At the moment, she was full-up on awful. "What is it?"

"We've never discussed it, but I want you to know I was wrong about you." He sipped from his cup, then continued. "You probably already know after what happened to you in Phoenix, I thought hiring you would be a mistake."

Now he was dissatisfied with her work? Where was this coming from? "Excuse me?"

"Let me finish."

"Get to it then, because I'm getting less content the longer it's taking you."

"Don't get me wrong. Your qualifications are sterling. But I didn't think for a second you'd stick with us for the long haul."

"Why not?"

"You're young and beautiful, and life here is tranquil. Honestly, I thought a woman as vibrant as you would get bored and move on at the end of the first school year."

"Do you want me to quit? Is that what this is about?"

"Lord, no!" His expression went from exasperated to horrified and then sobered. "In my own clumsy way, I am trying to admit I was wrong. It's difficult, okay? I haven't had a lot of practice—and I'm not bragging, just saying that's the way it's worked out." He paused, gathered his thoughts and then continued. "You were the perfect choice to run the school here. I'm thrilled you've stayed. We've been a blue-ribbon school every single year, and with all this… I had no idea how badly we'd need your skills as an innovator or as a psychologist. You've done an amazing job. That's all I was trying to say."

"Well, thank you, Thomas." Dana hadn't expected that, and she calmed down. "And your being wrong about me is not a problem. Truthfully, back then I would have been skeptical of me, too."

"Why?"

"Because I was still processing everything that had happened. I hadn't worked through it all in my mind yet."

"That's understandable even for us non-psychologists. Yours was a traumatic experience, Dana."

It had been traumatic. And heartbreaking. And terrifying. "Yes."

He refilled his coffee from the carafe and then topped off her cup. "And it's gracious of you not to rub my nose in being wrong."

"Don't give me too much credit." She parked her cup. "I've had tons of experience at being underestimated."

"Seriously?"

She nodded. "Most of my life. It happens when you earn dual Ph.D. degrees at the ripe old age of nineteen."

"That, I wouldn't know." He smiled. "So may I ask you something?" He focused beyond the glowing light and out into the darkness. "Why do you stay in Shutter Lake?"

"For the same reason I came here." She shrugged. "I feel safe… or I did, until recently."

He rubbed at his folded knee. "So Sylvia's murder rattled you, too."

"Of course. It's rattled everyone." Everyone else expected her to remain calm and collected. They expected the same from Thomas. But his expecting her to remain unaffected surprised her. If anyone knew we all need someone to just be ourselves with, it should be him. In that regard, they were kindred spirits.

"You are right, of course," he said. "Yet you carry it so well."

Now he'd lost her. "Carry what well?"

"The burden of being worried sick about more problems and crises coming up but appearing on the outside as if everything is firmly under control. You inspire me on that. I struggle with it."

"It doesn't show."

"Really?" His eyes widened.

She nodded. "Thomas, you're the most together person I've ever known. Perfection personified."

"Too much of it, eh?"

"Well," she scrunched her nose, "maybe just a little."

"My perfectionism is over the top. I know it." The skin between his eye brows wrinkled. "But the council… Their expectations are so high and precise."

The founders' council designed and built and remained the ultimate decision-makers on all things Shutter Lake. Thomas was right about them. Their expectations were high, precise and explicit. And not optional. The council could be amazingly generous or viciously brutal. This community was their sandbox, and if you wanted to play in it, you played by their rules. "Regardless," Dana said. "You are the mayor they've chosen but you're also a human being. You're entitled to a life. The life you want to have."

He sent her a sidelong look. "You know as well as I do what happens to those who oppose the council."

"Yes, I do." She'd seen it repeatedly. "But sometimes they do bend."

"When?" Thomas grunted. "I haven't seen it."

Dana met and held his gaze. "You haven't tested it."

"And you have?"

"Actually, yes. I have." She turned to face him. "Do you remember the house on Shutter Lake?"

"The one they offered you as a signing bonus when you came here to run the school. Sure, I do."

"Why do you think I refused to live there and moved into my cottage instead?"

"I have no idea." He clearly thought that had been a puzzling decision on her part.

"Because I like my cottage."

"The location of the lake house was the best in the community, and that house itself was totally awesome," he reminded her. "At least three times the size of your cottage."

"More. It sprawled forever. But this is where I wanted to live." She hiked a shoulder. She had felt fragile and small, and surrounded by all that space in the lake house made her feel more fragile and vulnerable, even smaller. The cottage had been perfect. "I saw this place, and it felt like home."

"And you insisted on this place—a deal-breaker, you said—and they didn't go ballistic on you for disagreeing with them."

"Exactly. Where I live is my choice."

He paused to think that through, and then finally responded. "So what you're saying is I should do more of what makes me feel like home, and like I'm living my life my way, than I am doing what they want or expect me to do?"

"Yes, I am."

He grunted. "You know, I know these things, but you get sucked into going along to get along and before you know it, it's all their way and you can't find more than specks of your own way anymore."

"So change that. I'm not saying to go crazy with changes, but to assess what they want and what you want. If something matters greatly to you, say so."

"Reclaim myself."

She nodded. "It's time, Thomas."

"You're not going to leave us, are you?" He whirled his finger. "I mean, because of this...event."

Sylvia's murder. "Never crossed my mind."

Relief washed across his face. "I know we have to find Sylvia's killer to ever be peaceful again. But McCabe and Holt will do that. I'm glad you'll be here."

"Me, too."

"And at the risk of upsetting you—which I do not want to do, especially after such a fantastic dinner—you do realize…"

"What?"

He started to answer and then changed his mind and said something else. "It's just, I'm worried about you. I'd feel better if I knew you accepted that Vinn killed Sylvia, and you're just proving it to yourself beyond a shadow of a doubt."

"Except Vinn didn't kill her."

The hope in Thomas's eyes died. "Why would he confess, then?"

"I might be able to answer that question if you'd let me talk to him."

"Dana, we discussed this earlier. You know I can't step on McCabe and Holt's toes."

But he wanted to step in, and she sensed that clearly. "I do understand." She said and meant it. After Laney's warning not to interfere today, how could Dana deny understanding? So much as a mention from Thomas would do nothing more than create tension between him and McCabe and Laney.

Whatever Thomas's beta moment was about, clearly he wasn't ready to talk it over. Julia's words at the press conference came back to Dana. *Hiding in plain sight.* "I hated seeing Connie Bradshaw breakdown like that. It was horrible."

"It was." A tremble haunted his tone. "Vernon got her home and settled in. Dr. Perez expects she'll sleep through the night."

Maybe, but she was going to wake up, and her nightmare would still be there. "And what happens tomorrow?"

"I don't know."

Oh, that look of his spoke volumes. Resentment and regret, and guilt. This was the beta-moment topic. Now, to get him to talk about it. "You were one of Connie's students back when she taught at Grass Valley High, weren't you?"

"Senior year." He quickly masked what were clearly fond memories. "She was a good teacher."

Dana recognized that adoring look. "You had a crush on her."

"Me and half the guys in school. It's a common thing for kids to crush on their favorite teacher."

"It is." Dana smiled. "Back in my classroom days, I was brought flowers, apples, and even a pet frog."

"A pet frog?" Thomas looked surprised.

"Not just any frog. This frog was that boy's prized possession. He loved that frog, and he wouldn't give it to just anyone." She turned tender. "It was Valentine's Day."

"Ah, true love." Thomas smiled and then sobered. "Isn't it a shame we lose that wonder?"

"Yes, it is. But isn't everything a wonder when you're six years old?"

"I didn't mean love. I meant ideal love." Thomas loosened his tie. "After the big first crush, you never again feel it in quite the same way."

"Some people do."

"I haven't. Have you?"

"No. Honestly, I haven't…yet."

"Hope springs eternal?"

She lifted a hand. "Why not?"

"I've never even come close to feeling that magic again." His expression clouded. "It sounds kind of strange to say, but I hope Sylvia did."

"Not strange at all. I hope she did, too," Dana said, a little wistful. "It'd be awful to be as full of life as she was and to die never having been loved."

"Her parents loved her."

"That's different. That's unconditional love, not ideal love."

"True." Thomas chewed on that a second, then said, "You know, I can't see that not knowing ideal love would bother Sylvia Cole."

"How could it not bother her?"

"She was different, Dana. Sylvia was determined to never need anyone for anything."

"Sounds like maybe she was once loved and things went badly. Someone break her heart?"

"Maybe. I don't know."

"Were you two close at some time?" Something was there. Dana felt it as if it were a tangible thing between them.

"No. She did my house," he said. "We'd talk now and then. That's as far as it went."

His tone said he hadn't wanted their relationship to go as far as it did, which brought Laney's question to Nolan Ikard at Stacked to mind. Dana let out a little, "Hmm."

"What?" he asked.

"In your talks, did Sylvia mention she'd planned a trip to Venezuela?"

"She mentioned it a couple of weeks ago." He paused, as if replaying the memory of their conversation. "I can't say she seemed excited about it. She called it an extended vacation, but she didn't act like it was a getaway. She seemed more resolved to go."

"I thought the same thing."

That confused him, so Dana explained. "She dropped by a few weeks ago after Yoga class at the Community Gathering Center to see my South American mask collection."

"You have masks from Venezuela?"

"A few. Actually, they're from all over South America. Venezuela, Brazil, Peru, and Argentina. I have a couple from Africa also." It was hard to believe a decade had passed since she'd been to Africa. "I used to love to travel."

"Really?" He hadn't expected that. "You haven't left Shutter Lake since you moved here."

"No, I haven't. But there was a time in my life when school would end one day and the next I'd take off for somewhere exotic and stay gone all summer." She smiled. "I've traveled all over the world."

"You must have loved it."

"I did. Every day was an adventure."

35

"Then why did you stop?"

Small and vulnerable. Afraid. Maybe if she'd travelled that first summer after Phoenix...but she hadn't. Just the idea of it had put her into cold chills. After that first year, it had been easier to avoid traveling than to summon the courage to do it. So she hadn't. She licked at her lips. "For the same reason I moved here."

"Phoenix?" He guessed.

She nodded. "I need to feel safe."

"Twenty-two kids, right?"

The school shooting. A lump rose in her throat. She fought to swallow it. "Thirteen injured. Nine dead. Four from my Kindergarten class." The horrors in that day stained her mind, tormented her soul. It bled fresh terror and tears. "We were all lined up single-file, walking to the lunchroom when it started..." Blasts of gunfire replayed in her mind. The screaming. Kids falling to the floor, lying in pools of their own blood. "We were in this stretch of the hallway with nowhere to go to get out of the line of fire." She blew out a sharp breath. "The shooter kept firing and turned away to fire behind him. He had his back to us, and the janitor's closet wasn't far. I grabbed two of the kids and motioned to the others to come. But by then three were dead."

"I thought you said four of your students died."

"I did." Dana swallowed hard. "One was down, injured but still breathing. I scooped her up and carried her with me to the closet. She died there." In Dana's arms, worried about leaking blood on Dana's skirt.

"I'm so sorry."

"Me, too." Memories of that day still haunted her. Finally, last summer, she'd put away the photo collage she'd made of herself with those four children. It'd taken all this time to put the horrors of that day in her past. Now, they were back. Disturbing and rearing all the demons she'd thought had finally been laid to rest.

"Dana, I can't imagine losing four students," Thomas said, then placed his hand over hers. The heat felt good, warming the icy chill that had set into her bones. "But you saved fourteen of your students that day because you thought fast and got those kids to safety."

"Logically, I know that." Her smile trembled. "But it's the ones you lose that keep you awake at night."

"And destroy your thirst for adventure."

"Changes it," she corrected him. "The greatest adventure for me now is making sure my students are protected and safe—and that includes Vinn Bradshaw. It might make you feel better to think he's guilty, Thomas, but I know that boy, and I'm telling you, he's innocent."

"Is he? Or do you need to believe he is because you can't bear the thought of losing another student?"

It was a fair question. One she couldn't honestly answer.

His phone rang, sparing her from having to try. "It's Zion," he said. "I have to take it."

"Of course." All that could be said about the mass shooting in Phoenix had been said. And all that could be felt had been felt by her ever since it occurred. Zion Cole, the extremely successful global investment analyst who never stinted when asked for community money, was a respected founder in Shutter Lake. When he called, everyone answered. Especially since he was grieving the loss of his only daughter, Sylvia.

Thomas stepped away. "I see," he said. "Well, if it's the only time everyone can get together, it's the only time everyone can get together. No problem. Where? All right. Give me fifteen minutes."

Thomas pocketed his phone and then turned to Dana. "I'm sorry, I'm going to have to go. Zion and the council want to discuss the renovations to City Hall."

"And this is the only time they can all make it. Sorry, I heard. I suspect Zion is trying to do anything normal or ordinary to take his mind off Sylvia."

"I guess that's normal. He looks awful, but who wouldn't?"

"Very normal. When our emotions are out of control, we seek comfort in the mundane minutiae. Doing everyday things occupies our minds and gives us a break from the debilitating grief." Dana stood up. "I'll walk you out then."

37

"Let me help you with these things." Thomas placed the cups and carafe on the tray with the remnants of the cheesecake cups.

"I can get that."

"It's done." Carrying the tray, Thomas breezed past her into the cottage, then slid the loaded tray onto the bar. "Thanks for dinner. The Mongolian was awesome."

"Oh, what about our discussion? You wanted to talk to me about something…your beta moment." Connie Bradshaw was the topic, but what exactly had he wanted to share?

"It'll have to wait. How about I make up for the eat-and-run by taking you to dinner?"

"Sure. That'd be great."

"This was easy, Dana."

"Easy?"

"Relaxing. Fun. You know what I mean."

Unfortunately, she did. "I do. And I'm glad. For me, too, Thomas."

He stepped outside. "Good night, then."

"Good night." She smiled. "Beta moment top of the agenda next dinner."

He nodded. "Absolutely."

Dana watched him go. No way would that discussion be had at or after their next dinner. She folded her arms across her chest, hearing his vehicle roar to life. They would probably never have that discussion. In the office, he had been ready to open up and talk about it. But by tonight, he'd had second thoughts.

And, if Thomas remained true to Thomas, that beta moment had come and gone and would not be revisited again.

So he'd had a thing for Connie. Maybe that's why he was so turned off to loving anyone. Not that any woman could ever compete with a high school boy's vision of his ideal love.

Grateful she wasn't in love with the man, Dana closed the door and locked up.

Chapter 5

Dana knew.

Thomas put the car in Drive, and pulled away from her cottage. She had to know or she wouldn't have asked him about Connie. He swallowed hard. His first love. . .and probably his last.

Forbidden.

His stomach clenched. Yes, she had been his teacher. Yes, it had been wrong, but neither of them had intended to fall in love. It had just happened…

An unexpected whirlwind romance that had been exciting and adventurous, and definitely forbidden. When they could both sneak away, they would meet at the old mine and talk and make love.

It had been the best and, in retrospect, the worst, thing that had happened to him in his whole life. He had fallen for her so hard, and no other woman had ever made him feel all she had made him feel. No one claimed every beat of his heart or scorched his soul and made him yearn for more. Even now, he would give anything, everything he would ever have, for just five more minutes of what they had shared then. Just five more minutes….

Long before he was ready for things to end, he showed up at

school one day and—*boom*—she was gone. He'd been afraid to ask too many questions. Three of the longest days ever, wondering what had happened to her, why she had left, passed. Then, he heard she had married Vernon Bradshaw and she wouldn't be coming back to teach at Grass Valley High anymore.

Connie. Married. To another man. Thomas's stomach clenched and hollowed now as it had the first time he had heard the news. He had been totally devastated in the way only a boy crazy in love with an older woman who just had lost her to a rich, older man could be devastated.

Braking at the stoplight, Thomas felt again his determination rise. Never again would he come second to any man. Never again.

He had graduated high school then college, made his fortune and inherited another one, and then he had returned to Grass Valley to decide which mountain to tackle next to further prove his personal worth. If he happened to see regret she'd chosen the wrong man on Connie Bradshaw's face, so much the better.

He'd seen her surprise, but not her regret...yet. Shutter Lake was in development then, so when Zion Cole approached Thomas on behalf of the council and asked him to run for mayor, he had accepted.

Turning off Old Mine Road toward Zion's mansion on the lake, Thomas let himself remember the day he first had seen Connie again. It had been about three months after her marriage to Vernon Bradshaw.

Actually, it'd been two months, twelve days and four hours.

She'd been sitting on a sidewalk bench outside the drug store in Grass Valley. Thomas had hesitated, unsure if he should speak to her, but the town was small and avoiding anyone indefinitely wasn't going to happen, so he walked up and stopped to say hello. They talked for a couple of minutes about innocuous, trivial things, then she stood up and he saw the reason for her rushed marriage. Connie was pregnant.

His knees had nearly buckled and his stomach seized. He buried his shock, keeping it all inside, but he wondered. *His or mine?* She said nothing about it. Not a single word.

After the most awkward silence of his life, they exchanged bane pleasant farewells, and she walked away. A thousand questions racing through his mind, he watched her go. Dropped down onto the bench she had vacated, and battled with himself. Why hadn't he asked her? *Why?*

But he already knew why he hadn't asked. For the same reason he hadn't asked in the hundreds of times he had seen her since: He didn't want to know.

Back then, he had plans. He was going off to college and to make something of himself, and she was married to another man. The wrong man. If Thomas had asked the question then, he would know the truth now, but he was seventeen years old. What seventeen year old with plans would dare touch that question. It was a sharp and unforgiving double-edged sword.

If his suspicions proved true, Thomas would have had to do something. The right thing. Even then he'd known that would have been disastrous for his future, for her and for her child's futures, and for Vernon. Thomas couldn't compete with Vernon Bradshaw. He couldn't give Connie all that a rich and successful investor could give her. Thomas loved her, but he couldn't be the kind of husband or father she and her baby deserved. One day, that would change. But at seventeen that day hadn't yet arrived.

A lot changed the morning Vinn had been born. The temptation to just see him had been too great to resist. Late that night, Thomas had sneaked into the hospital to get a glimpse of him—not that Connie or anyone else ever knew it. And as the years had passed and Vinn had grown and Thomas had seen the boy around town, he'd continued to wonder. He took to photographing Vinn early on, and to comparing those photos to ones of himself at Vinn's age. Year after year, Thomas would compare and the result was always the same. They could have been twins.

Once, the year Vinn had been Joseph in the church Christmas program—more for his height than his acting ability—Thomas had almost succumbed and asked Connie if he was Vinn's father. But then Vernon had taken his seat at her side and Thomas had seen the way they sat with their heads together, whispering about Vinn and his performance, and they looked so happy. Thomas felt like an intruder. He had been an intruder. And he hadn't said a word.

What good could come from knowing? They were a family, and inserting himself, he would just mess that up for all of them. He couldn't do it. He wouldn't do it.

Regaining his resolve, Thomas drove around the rim of the lake to Zion Cole's home, pulled in to the circle drive parking, and then cut the engine. Depleted and exhausted was the penalty he paid for thinking back to those tumultuous times. And at the moment, he felt the heavy weight of both. Connie and Vernon had made a good life together. Thomas was the outsider then and now. He didn't belong. He'd forfeited any right to belong the day he had discovered she was pregnant and had said nothing.

He had chosen not to ask.

He closed his eyes, thought back to today, at the press conference. The memory of Connie's screams, her soul-torn desperation, ripped through his chest. Her marriage had endured, and yet today, when Connie and Vinn had most needed Vernon, he had stood outside City Hall in the middle of all those people like a zoned-out addict instead of going inside and trying to comfort his wife. Even from the lower steps outside, Thomas had heard Connie screaming, and Vinn yelling, begging for them to get her out of there. Yet Vernon hadn't moved until summoned.

Dana knew. But how?

Sylvia. Thomas's mind raced. She must have told Dana about Connie. God knew Thomas had never told a soul in his life, but Sylvia had threatened to tell people. Everyone, actually. It had cost Thomas a small fortune to buy her silence.

He couldn't do what he was tempted to do: toss her out on her blackmailing ear. Connie and Vinn would have been hurt most, and Sylvia knew it. Thomas had to care because of the stringent requirements the council put on him and his image. But that was a gnat-sized concern. Connie and Vinn were dragonflies. So Thomas had bought Sylvia's silence to protect them. That heartless woman would ruin their lives and never look back, or blink twice.

Thomas rubbed at his jaw, remembering the day the blackmail had begun. He'd spilled iced tea on his shirt at lunch and had gone home to switch to a fresh one before a meeting with the council. Sylvia had been there, in his bedroom, and she had the photos of him and Vinn splayed across his bed...

She heard him enter and looked up at him, her long blond hair hugging her cheek. "Well, aren't you the sly one?" Her smile was cold and calculating.

"What are you doing?" He barely leashed his outrage. "Why are you going through my things?"

Pinching two photographs between her forefingers and thumbs, she hiked a shoulder. "I'm your housekeeper, Thomas. It's my job to tidy your things."

Fury burned his stomach. "Not anymore." He wagged a finger at the photos. "Put those down and go. You're fired, Sylvia."

She didn't move. Or drop the photos. "You might want to rethink that, Mayor. It never pays to be rash...unless you're ready to lose the election and be forced out of Shutter Lake."

"You're blackmailing me?" He couldn't believe it. How could she be so brazen and merciless?

"Of course not. Blackmail is illegal, and such a nasty word." She batted her mascaraed lashes. "I prefer cooperation assistance."

He wanted to smack her. He wanted to tell her to get out and tell anyone she wanted. But this wasn't just about him. It was about Connie and Vinn, and Vernon, too. Did he know or even suspect Vinn wasn't his?

Didn't matter. They would all still pay the heaviest price for Thomas giving in to his temper. "How much is your cooperation assistance going to cost me?"

She named a sum. "And I want Sparkle named Business of the Year."

"Your cleaning service won the award last year," he reminded her, wondering who she'd blackmailed for it then.

"I want it again." Her deep red lips settled into a pout. "No one has won it two years in a row before. I want Sparkle to be the first."

"Sylvia, I only have one vote on that board. The entire chamber has a voice."

"Then I suggest you use your charm to convincingly persuade others." She held up the photos. "Unless you want these spread around town."

Thomas accepted defeat. For himself, he'd fight her. But for Connie and Vinn, he'd pay the devil's dues. "I'll do what I can."

"So tell me. Does he know?" She nodded toward the photo of Vinn. "Does Connie know you photograph him?"

"Of course he doesn't know." Thomas frowned. "I'm not sure myself."

"Ah, I see." She smiled. "She never told you. But she was naughty, sleeping with a student."

That infuriated Thomas. "Get out, Sylvia. Just go."

"No problem." She dropped the photos and stood up. "Two o'clock Friday. Have the money delivered to Sparkle by then, or at three o'clock…"

"Just get out."

"THOMAS?"

Hard raps fell against Thomas's car window, pulling him and his attention back to his sitting parked in Zion Cole's driveway.

From the other side of the glass, Zion waved. "Thomas, are you all right in there?"

Thomas sucked in a sharp breath, let it out slowly. His "maybe son" in jail for murder, his "perfect" town in an emotional uproar over the death of his blackmailer, the love of his life still happily married to another man, and—his responsibility—the illusion of Shutter Lake as the safest and most idyllic community in the country shattered. No, he was not okay. He most definitely was not okay.

Thomas forced himself to smile and opened the car door. "I'm fine, Zion." He stepped out and extended his hand, shook Zion's. "Gathering my thoughts. That's all."

Unfortunately, most of them centered on the mess Zion Cole's black-hearted daughter had made of their town, getting herself killed....

Chapter 6

Tuesday, October 9

THE "EXPRESS YOURSELF" assembly proved as necessary as Dana feared it might. The uproar at the press conference had impacted the parents sufficiently to pass along their anxieties to their kids and now, from five to seventeen, here they all sat lined up on rows of bleachers in the gym with Dana standing front and center before them, reassuring them for the past fifteen minutes that they were safe. Hopefully, now they were ready to settle down. Their nervous twitches, itching, bouncing feet and wringing hands had lessened and fewer looked as tense and wary as frightened cats, so signs were good. Hopeful, she dared to ask, "Everyone okay?"

Kristina Sharapova, the Windermere's Russian exchange student, raised her hand. Her typically serious expression looked tighter and her eyes clouded. "I'm not okay, Dr. Perkins."

Dana wished Vinn were here. He'd calm Kristina; she trusted him. Quentin and Katherine Windermere weren't prone to anxiety. If they were, the childless couple would never have hosted so many exchange students. At least one per year. Sometimes, two. And with the exception of the one who had worked part-time at Sparkle, Sylvia's housecleaning service, for a few months...

What was that child's name? Josie. Josie Rodriguez. Beautiful girl. A junior, and very bright. What had happened to her? Dana made a mental note to check into that. Exchange students worked so hard to get to the States to study, much less into Shutter Lake. To throw away the opportunity due to a family emergency seemed senseless. Dana had expected Josie back in a few days and instead Katherine Windermere had notified the office Josie wouldn't be returning. The girl was gone. That much Dana knew for sure. She hadn't caught wind of her being seen in Shutter Lake since her departure.

"Dr. Perkins?" Kristina prodded.

Dana focused on the girl now standing in place near the top of the bleachers. "Why are you not okay, Kristina?" Softening her tone, Dana smiled. "What exactly is wrong?"

"There's a killer loose and I'm scared," she said. "We all are."

A chorus of voices rose in agreement. Some were those of staff members. Dana frowned at them, then addressed the kids. "Fear is a normal response. You act as if it is a bad thing, but fear can be a good thing, too."

"How?" Kristina asked.

"Well, it can make you more aware. Fear can warn you of things so you can protect yourself."

"Like what?" A third-grader asked.

"Let's say you're standing before a hot stove. You feel the heat. That heat warns you that the stove is hot, right? Of course, it does. You don't have to touch the stove to know it's hot. You're afraid to touch it because it is hot, and because you are, you don't touch the stove and get burned." She cited a few other examples of how fear can be a good thing, targeting the different age groups so all the students had a relatable example to apply in their own lives. "So you see, fear isn't a bad thing. Like most things, fear can be constructive or destructive. It's how you look at it, and how you handle it. That's what's important."

More and more faces relaxed and tensions eased. Dana let them ask their questions, and answered them honestly, giving them constructive coping skills. And though it galled her to do it, she reminded them, "Vinn has confessed and he is secured."

Relaying those facts was hard for her because with every atom in her body, she believed he was innocent.

"Why would he do that?" Kristina asked Dana. "Why would he confess to a crime he didn't commit?"

A freshman new to Shutter Lake seated near Wade Travis, the history teacher, stood up. "Did Vinn do it? Everybody knows he didn't trust Sylvia."

Kristina pounced, responding before Dana could. "Of course, he didn't do it. You know, Vinn. We all know he couldn't do something like that."

Kristina sounded more than certain. She sounded positive. How could she have no doubt? And what in the world had Wade Travis suddenly turning the sickly color of ash?

"He said he did." The red-faced boy sat back down. "Vinn don't usually lie."

"I know what he said. That doesn't make it so." Kristina turned to Dana. "Does it, Dr. Perkins?"

"No, it doesn't," she admitted. "And that proves how important it is that we all just tell the truth."

Kristina stood up yet again. "Can we go now?"

"Provided everyone is okay, yes." Grateful for the reprieve, Dana took another look then motioned to the history teacher. "Mr. Travis?" Since Sylvia's murder, he'd been walking around looking a little lost and a lot frightened. Dana had asked him why several times, but he'd brushed off her concerns, insisting he was fine. Whatever was going on with him, it was time to find out. No one that uptight could be a calming influence on the students.

They began exiting the gym to return to class and Wade Travis joined Dana. A little pudgy, he parked a hand on his stomach. "I had my doubts about these touchy-feely assemblies, but they seem to be working."

"Listening to the students is always a powerful help." Dana and he stepped aside. "How has Kristina been doing in class?"

Mr. Travis tapped his glasses at the bridge of his broad nose, then dragged a thoughtful hand over his balding pate. "Jittery. Scared. She's been even more upset since Vinn confessed." Mr. Travis frowned. "I don't know if it is her inbred fear of authorities or what actually happened with Sylvia and now Vinn being in the middle of it, but something has her pretty spooked."

And him also, Dana thought, gauging by the breaks in his voice and his stilted tones.

"Vinn is her closest friend, so I guess the nerves are about him, and to be expected."

"Are the other students treating her well?"

"For the most part," Travis said. "A few are distant because of the whole killer thing. Everyone knows she and Vinn are best friends, so I guess that's pretty normal, too—the distancing themselves, I mean. But most of them have known Vinn forever, and they don't believe he could kill...her."

Mr. Travis refused to say Sylvia's name. How odd.

The majority of the kids had left the gym. Keeping her voice down so it wouldn't carry, Dana faced Mr. Travis squarely. "What is wrong with you?"

"What?" His face flushed, at odds with his words. "Nothing's wrong with me. I—I mean, nothing that isn't wrong with everyone around here."

"Mr. Travis... Wade," Dana lowered her voice another notch. "I simply don't have the time or energy to be anything but blunt and direct. You've been acting strange since Sylvia's murder. Now, stop with the avoidance tactics and just be honest with me. What is wrong?" Maybe they had been close, or he had some unknown connection to the family. Whatever it was, he needed to get a grip on it. How could he help calm the kids when his every nerve was stretched as tight as strung wire?

His jaw tightened then fell slack, and he hesitated a long moment, suddenly looking far older and more weary than his thirty-two years. Worry aged a man more than anything else could.

Eventually the staring match ended, and he responded. "What's wrong? Well, my star student is in jail for murder, the rest of my students have the focus span of gnats, and my nerves aren't in much better shape than theirs. Other than that, everything is great."

Sylvia had cleaned his house, too, and he seemed profoundly affected by her loss. "I see." Dana nodded, confirmed that she really did see far more than he intended to show her. He was struggling and needed help. "No doubt you and Sylvia chatted. We did, too," Dana added. "Did she mention she was planning a trip to Venezuela?"

He stiffened and stopped himself from backing away from Dana. "Did she tell you that? Who told you that?"

Definitely an over-reaction to a non-personal question. The straggling students stopped and stared. Dana smiled to let them know all was well and then shooed them. "Get on to class or you'll be late."

The cluster of three girls and two boys hustled to the gym door. When it closed behind them, Dana looked back at Wade Travis. As a member of her staff, he too fell under her protection. Whether or not he wanted it, he apparently had been profoundly impacted by Sylvia's death and needed it. "At the end of the day, come to my office."

"I'm sorry, Dr. Perkins. Really. I—"

"Right after classes, Mr. Travis." Dana walked out of the gym.

Chapter 7

Wade entered the faculty restroom, grateful he had a break before his next class. His insides shook so hard, he was surprised half his guts and all his breakfast weren't already on the floor.

Right after classes, Mr. Travis.

She knew.

He looked into the mirror above the sink, disgusted by his own reflection. What was he going to do? He could lie, but Perkins would know. She had too many years in the classroom and around kids to not have a honed BS detector.

How did she find out? He'd been so careful. Meticulously careful…

Sylvia. She was the only other person on the planet that knew his secret. The only one. The day she had confronted him roared through his mind. Sylvia had waited for the kids to leave his classroom and clear the hall. Then she'd walked in and slammed his door shut. "I did your house today, Wade."

"You do my house every Thursday." To avoid her glare, he picked up an eraser and began making circles on the board, getting rid of a few notes.

"Porn?" She was furious. "Stop that and look at me."

He had to struggle to make his body move, awash in a hot flood of shame. He set down the eraser, took a steadying breath, steeling himself, and then turned to face her.

"I found your stash." Sylvia parked a hand on her hip. "And I'll tell you right now, if there had been little kids in that mountain of trash and not grown women—though that's bad, no doubt about it —we wouldn't be having this conversation. You'd be with Griff McCabe in cuffs and on your way to jail."

"Sylvia, don't. Please." His stomach pitched and rolled and spots formed before his eyes. "Please."

"Please?" Are you crazy? Porn? You're a teacher, for God's sake."

Why didn't she lower her voice? Someone was going to hear. He lifted a hand and pumped the air, silently asking her to pipe down. "It's an addiction," he told Sylvia. "I have never and will never touch a kid. That's disgusting."

"These women you watch. They're acting of their own free will?"

"Yes." He lied. Some of them were, but others... he couldn't be so sure. And one, he doubted very seriously was there of her own volition. She'd been drugged to the rafters the first time he'd seen her. Not so much in the times since, but...

"Okay, then." Sylvia paced a few steps between the rows of desks. "Since they're acting of their own free will, I'm going to let you buy my cooperative assistance. You give me a reasonable sum of money for my silence and you get to keep your job. And your occasional dates with Heidi Udall, too." She stopped suddenly and glared at him. "But if I ever hear even one rumor you've done anything with a kid, I'm going straight to McCabe and reporting you for porn. That's the best you're getting from me. Take it or leave it."

A chance. She was giving him a chance to keep his life. "How much?"

She named a sum and they haggled but she had him by the short hairs, no denying it, so he settled. He couldn't do it, however, without a threat. "All right. All right, Sylvia," he told her. "I'll do what you want, but you better remember one thing."

"What's that?"

"You ever tell anyone, and I mean anyone, and you're going to regret it. I swear it."

"What an amateur." Her lackluster reaction fell far short of his expectations. She wasn't frightened, she smiled. "You need a better argument, rookie. I've been threatened by the best. They always give in before I give up." She stepped closer and leaned in. "Threaten me again, and the days of my silence are over. Oh, did I mention I've got proof? Well, I do. Not at my house, of course, so don't think about breaking in and retrieving it. I've got it stored safely elsewhere. You behave, it stays tucked away." She rolled her gaze toward the clouds. "But if anything happens to me... You won't like it. It'll trigger a dead man's switch."

"A dead man's switch?" His mouth turned dust-dry. "You seriously expect me to believe that?"

"I seriously don't care what you believe, pervert. A triggered switch means I'll be dead," she reminded him. "But you'll be alive and right here, and everyone on the planet will see exactly who you are and what you've been up to, so even if I lose, I win. You, on the other hand, lose everything." She shot him a warning glare. "Remember that, and don't threaten me again ever. It annoys me." She dipped her chin, shot him a look that could melt ice. "And don't forget what I said about the kids."

Without another word, Sylvia left his classroom and softly closed the door.

Standing in the faculty restroom, Wade's stomach pitched and rolled. At the sink, he slapped at the spigot, splashed cold water on his face and rubbed briskly, his hands shaking uncontrollably. Not only had Sylvia known his dirty secret, she had proof of it stored in some unknown cloud. Worse, since her death, he'd feared her dead man's switch had triggered and every second of every day would be *the* second his darkest shame would be exposed. The proof would appear everywhere, revealed for all to see. Everyone would know. Perkins. The council. His neighbors. Heidi. The kids...

What if Sylvia's switch had already been triggered? What if the proof had gone straight to Dr. Perkins?

Sylvia might have done that. She was concerned about protecting the kids from him. He was into porn, not kids. Addicted, not perverted. He ripped off a bunch of paper towels from the dispenser and swiped at his face.

He vomited twice, rinsed his mouth and, still in a cold sweat, he staggered back to his classroom. Dr. Perkins had been concerned. If she knew anything, she never would have let him return to class. But if Sylvia had done what she threatened, soon everyone would know. People wouldn't understand. They'd look at him and see a disgusting pervert teaching their kids. He'd lose his job, his house, his life. And there was nothing he could do about it but wait and watch it happen. Dr. Perkins wanted to see him.

Right after classes...

Chapter 8

Dana girded her proverbial loins and then reached behind her office desk for her tote. Last night, the nightmares of Phoenix had returned with a vengeance and she had given into the urge, pulled the photo collage of the four students she had lost from her dresser drawer, and studied their sweet faces. Cara, Misty, Sara and Joshua. Clutching the frame to her chest, she had wept and wept until she cried herself back to sleep.

This morning, she had promised them yet again that she would protect the students entrusted to her care. First and foremost and always. She'd cried again, showered and dressed in a gold silk blouse and black skirt and then had come to work, ready to do whatever she had to do to keep that promise.

Her stomach still rumbled its discontent. She pulled out the photo and studied their familiar faces, their innocent smiles. Acid burned in her stomach. She set the photo on her desk then reached for the roll of antacids in her top desk drawer. Chewed one, then another. "Get it together, Dana," she whispered to herself. "Do what you have to do."

The students under her protection included Vinn. He needed

her at the top of her game as much as the angels in Phoenix had needed her back then. She had failed them. She would not fail her students again.

She would not fail Vinn.

Straightening in her seat, she pushed the intercom button to speak to her assistant, Pamela Clark, the formal and dedicated thirty-year-old woman she'd hired this school year to replace one more lax at following her instructions. Pam might be a little zealous, but she carried out Dana's requests with military precision, kept meticulous notes on everyone and everything, and she was harder on herself than Dana would ever be on her. Pam knew her job, her primary responsibilities and the thousand unspoken expectations placed on her. Not once had she fallen short.

"Pam?"

"Yes, Dr. Perkins."

"Please pull Kristina Sharapova from class and have her come to my office."

"Right away."

The antacid kicked in and the burn in Dana's stomach eased. Grateful for it, she glanced at the photo of Cara, Misty, Sara and Joshua. "No matter what it takes, I won't fail again," she promised, then tucked the photo back into her tote bag.

Minutes later, Pam appeared at the office door. "Kristina is here, Dr. Perkins."

"Show her in, please."

Kristina stepped into Dana's office, looking scared and uncomfortable. "Am I in trouble, Dr. Perkins?" She lowered her book bag to the floor and swiped her hair back behind her ear. "I'm sorry I shouted in assembly. I was nervous."

"You're fine, Kristina." Dana removed her reading glasses and motioned to a seat across from her desk. "Sit down, please."

Kristina lowered herself onto the chair and sat perched forward like a bird ready for flight. Her jaw trembled.

"It really is okay." Dana smiled. "You don't need to be worried."

She dragged her teeth over her lower lip. "I've never been

summoned to the principal's office. At home, the only kids who get summoned are the ones in trouble."

"That's not how it works at Shutter Lake." Dana smiled again. "I just wanted to make sure you're okay."

She nodded.

"And I wonder if you might help me with something, Kristina."

The thought that she might be able to help Dana clearly stunned her. "Me?"

Dana bobbed her head. "At assembly, you said Vinn didn't kill Sylvia."

She plucked at her slacks, seeking comfort in the feel of the fabric. "Yes."

"You seemed sure of it," Dana said.

"I am sure of it." Kristina's voice gained strength.

"Even though he says he did do it." Dana avoided the murder word, or the kill one.

Again, she nodded.

"Why would he do that—say he did it, if he hadn't done it?" Dana let Kristina see her worry. "I can't figure that out."

Frustration and confusion riddled Kristina's face. She let her gaze wander to the ceiling, obviously seeing something far beyond it in her mind. "I don't know. I've tried and tried to figure it out, but I just can't."

Dana sat back. "It doesn't make sense to me. I know he and Sylvia were friends. She helped him with his school project. Actually, it was about her and Sparkle. How she created the business."

"I remember. She was so successful. Vinn did a good job on that project, and she did help him with it." Kristina agreed. "But then they stopped being friends."

"They did?" Dana let out a little mumble. "I didn't realize that."

Kristina nodded, clearly bothered by that situation.

When she didn't continue, Dana nudged her. "Why? After working on the project together, I thought they'd keep on being friends."

"I don't know." Kristina rubbed her slacks harder, absently.

"Something happened and he didn't trust her anymore. He told me that. He said he'd been stupid to ever trust her."

"It must have been serious for Vinn to turn against her like that." Dana parked her elbow on her desk, cupped her chin. "I wonder what Sylvia did to make him so angry with her?"

"He wouldn't say. I asked a couple times, until he told me not to anymore. We talked about almost everything. But not about that." Kristina grunted her irritation at being shut out. "I know he was really ticked off. Though…"

"Though what?" Dana pushed.

Kristina looked back at Dana. "He wasn't really angry at her. Not like he wanted to hurt her or anything like that. He just didn't trust her anymore." Kristina shrugged. "She tried to talk to him a couple of times. I was there. But before she could get anywhere close to him, he yelled at her to go away and leave him alone."

"Vinn yelled at Sylvia?" Dana let out a grunt of her own. "Now that's odd. I've never known him to be rude to anyone."

Kristina lowered her voice, checked the door and, seeing it remained closed, she glanced back at Dana. "It was weird, Dr. Perkins. I told him so, too."

"What did he say?"

"That she deserved worse." Kristina blinked hard, as if the exchange had caused her to fear he had given her worse. No doubt that worry had created some sleepless nights. "I don't know what she did, but whatever it was, it totally pis—er, ticked-off Vinn. He didn't want anything to do with her."

"Yet you don't think he killed her."

"I know he didn't."

There it was again. That total certainty. "How do you know, Kristina?"

Her face blanked. Finally, she said, "I can't tell you. But I do know."

Dana softened her voice. "It's difficult to accept that people we care about can be good people and yet do bad things."

"It's not like that," she cut in. "I—I just know, okay? I just know."

58

"Okay." Dana paused for effect. "Kristina, I'm going to trust you." When she nodded, Dana went on. "I don't believe Vinn killed Sylvia either. But believing it, isn't enough. To get him out of this mess, we need to prove he's innocent."

"How do we prove it?" Kristina seemed willing to help but at a loss on how to do it.

Dana sat back, clasped her hands in her lap. "You can start with telling me how you know he didn't do it."

"I told you, I can't."

The desperation in her tone alerted Dana, and she asked the question she should have asked the first time. "You can't, or you won't?"

"What's the difference, Dr. Perkins?" Kristina looked ready to bolt. "Most likely, I know the same way you do. We know Vinn."

Whatever she knew she wasn't ready to share, and pushing her any harder would only alienate her into shutting down. "Well, you think about it," Dana pulled back, "and if you can somehow help me prove he didn't do this, I'd appreciate your help."

She nodded and grabbed her book bag. "If Vinn was mad enough to kill Sylvia Cole, he would have done it when he first got mad at her—don't you think?"

Crime of passion? "Maybe. But sometimes anger builds over time and it finally gets to people."

"I've never seen him as mad as he was at her at first. After that, when she'd try to talk to him, he'd gripe for her go away, but then once she left, he was okay. I mean, he let it go, you know?"

"That doesn't sound like anger building up to me."

The wrinkle between Kristina's brows faded. "It doesn't to me, either."

Dana smiled. "That's good news, then. Now if you think of anything else…"

"I'll let you know, Dr. Perkins." She slung her book bag over her shoulder and left the office fast.

Kristina Sharapova was a good friend to Vinn—as good a friend as he'd been to her, helping her settle in here. And she knew more than she was telling Dana.

Maybe, just maybe, Kristina would think about it all and share that missing information Dana needed to help Vinn. To protect him.

Starting with protecting him from himself.

Chapter 9

BREAKDOWN

After the talk with Kristina, Dana spoke with four different parents concerned about their children's safety. She thought of Gracie's cat, Patience, and considered borrowing it for the rest of the morning. If Dana weren't allergic, she might have asked, but a reaction and a delicate stomach that had steadily grown more fragile with each successive phone call nixed the idea.

She plucked her red-framed reading glasses from her desk and put them on then turned to her computer. A lot of people in Shutter Lake seemed to know about Sylvia's extended vacation, but the only one who seemed unnerved by her plans to visit Venezuela was Wade Travis. Why?

Dana keyed in an Internet search request on Venezuela at Duck-DuckGo.com, then scanned the results. "International Court looking into allegations of excessive force and other abuses." She sighed. "Government's a wreck." Looking on, she paused on the next item of interest. "U.S. travel restrictions." Why would Sylvia go there now when the State Department had issued an alert and travel was restricted? People were starving. Grocery store shelves were empty. "Not your typical vacation paradise at the moment." Dana kept looking. Her gaze slowed on the next article. "A source for commercial sexual exploitation and forced labor?"

Dana read the article, then sat back in her seat, her fingers pressed to her lips. "Number five in human trafficking. Number five?"

How in the world could there be a connection? Back when Dana had travelled to Venezuela, which was nearly a decade ago now, a lot of people who lived in the interior would come to the tourist attraction areas looking for work. Of course, a lot could have changed in that period of time. Why would Sylvia want to go there right now?

Back on the search page, Dana located an article that caught her eye and interest but it didn't answer her question. "U.S. State Department's Office to monitor and combat trafficking in persons placed the country in 'Tier 3' in 2017."

None of this was the Venezuela she had known. Dana's stomach flipped. Things had changed all right. They'd gotten worse. She leaned back in her seat and absorbed all she had read. Why would Sylvia go there at all, much less now? Why would she plan an extended stay? With so much turmoil throughout the country and those travel restrictions…

It didn't make sense. Sylvia wasn't stupid, and she wasn't flighty. Independent, yes, but clear-headed or she never would have built a successful business. She had been raised by Zion and Yolanda Cole, wealthy pharmaceutical tycoons, and she was privileged. But she never had been indulged—her choice, not Zion and Yolanda's. They would have given her anything. Sylvia wouldn't take it. She'd made her way on her own. Maybe to prove to them or to herself that she could. Regardless of her reasons, she had made her own way. That required good judgment and sense. A lifelong habit of exercising both. So why abandon those habits now, over this?

Dana had no answers, but she did have questions. Considering Wade Travis's reaction to Dana's questions about Sylvia and Venezuela in the gym, maybe he could shed some light on the subject. If he would. Oh, to be that deeply affected by her death, he could tell her plenty. Dana had sensed that clearly. He'd been acting strange since word of Sylvia's death had come out, and he'd reacted to Dana's questions in straight-up, self-defense mode. Far too defensive to not know something significant.

Who else might have some insights?

Gazing out through her office window, Dana let her mind wander through possibilities. *Too vague.* She homed in on a specific. What had she done before travelling to a foreign country? She tapped her fingertips against the edge of her desk. "Passport." Sylvia would have to update her passport. She hadn't taken a vacation since she'd opened Sparkle. Of course, it would need updating, which meant she'd need to see Ana. Anyone needing medical records checked for matters such as this had to visit Dr. Perez.

Feeling the burn in her stomach, Dana popped another antacid tablet into her mouth just as Pam stuck her head in the door. "Sorry to interrupt, Dr. Perkins. Dr. Perez wants you to drop by the medical clinic to get your labs done." Pam frowned. "She called herself, so I think this is your last warning."

Dana had been due for her annual physical—a contractual requirement with the council—for three months, and she had rescheduled a couple of times. But if Ana was calling herself, it meant the reprieve was over. Since it was a good opportunity to ask her about Sylvia, Dana seized it. "Well, I guess I'd better go do that right now, then."

Pam cast her a suspicious look. "Are you sick?"

"You know the labs are for the routine physical."

"Finally, you're going to do it." Relief swept across Pam's face. "Good. They've been nagging me to nag you for two months."

"Three."

"I was being generous." Pam wiggled a finger in Dana's direction. "Best not let the health-nut Nazi see you downing antacid then."

"Don't use that word, Pam. I won't have it." Dana frowned. "And I'll keep quiet about the antacid, though with the hornet's nest around here, I don't see how anyone is avoiding an acidic stomach."

"She'll have you in Yoga five nights a week, and we both know it."

Ana likely would. Dana logged out of her computer.

"I've been telling you for six months to back off those Macchiato Espressos from The Grind, but you come in every morning, carrying a cup." Pam returned to her desk.

"Guilty." And many of those mornings she had stood in line with Sylvia, who ordered a Green Tea with Chia Crème Frappuccino and a single chocolate croissant, except on Wednesdays. Then she always ordered an extra bagel or muffin. Dana had wondered for months why Sylvia's pattern changed only on Wednesday, and finally she'd asked.

"Oh, I bring a treat to Troy Duval," she'd said. "I do his house on Wednesday mornings."

Only select people in Shutter Lake knew Troy was a recluse who had been married to the famous actress, Madelyn Yates. According to Thomas, his name had been Jason Lavelle back then, and he and his family had lived in Los Angeles. But then his wife and daughter had been murdered. After the horrible story had played out in the news, Jason had changed his name to Troy Duval and moved to Shutter Lake, where he'd become the resident mysterious recluse. Everyone knew he was there, but few knew his history and all respected his privacy. In the past few years, Sylvia had changed his designation from recluse to shut-in. No one who knew his story knew why, but since Sylvia was about the only person who ever saw Troy, those aware of him thought little of the change.

Who brought him a bagel now? Dana reached into her bottom desk drawer for her handbag. Retrieved it, betting Renata Fernandez, who'd taken over cleaning for him, didn't. Poor man probably never saw anyone else.

Dana grabbed a pen and added him to her to-do list, then left her office. She paused at Pam's desk. "Thanks for caring and for taking the nagging."

"It's a job perk." She smiled.

"Well, I'm going to spare you any more of that perk for this year."

"Good idea since Dr. Perez is hot on your trail."

"Going to the medical clinic now to get the lab work taken care of. If the search party she sends for me arrives before I get back—"

"I'll let them know you crossed paths." Pam sighed. "It's the last part. She's done everything else. Just do it and get it over with."

"I know." Dana smiled. "I've been busy, okay?"

"Trust me, I know."

She did. When Dana was busy, Pam was busier. That's how it worked. "I appreciate you."

"Don't."

"Excuse me?" Dana came to a full stop.

"When you appreciate me, you stop at Batter Up and get cupcakes."

"But it's Tuesday," Dana said. "Heidi makes German Chocolate on Tuesdays. They're still your favorite, right?"

"This, you remember. Great." Pam guffawed. "I'm already doing an extra mile on the treadmill every morning, training up for the winter run. So you're threatening me with my favorite cupcakes."

"It wasn't a threat."

"My annual physical is in two weeks."

Shutter Lake was huge on healthy living and lifestyles. Most residents thought that was their own idea, but the truth was, the founders insisted on it and encouraged it in every way. "If you nag, I'm going to detour to Batter Up. That's a fact."

"It'd be my luck Sheena Appleton will be filling in for Heidi or something." She frowned, scrunching her nose. "It's not her blue hair that gets me. Lots of people in their twenties do that. It's wearing black all the time. Always brings funerals to mind."

"It's a fad. Comes and goes." It had several times in Dana's adult years, and likely would again.

"Sheena hasn't come over from Grass Valley as Heidi's backup baker since Heidi broke her wrist—and she's a good baker."

"Doesn't do German Chocolate cupcakes like Heidi."

"Who could?" Dana turned away.

Pam snagged Dana's sleeve. "I wouldn't mind if you'd bring me just one cupcake. But no more than that. Just one."

"You got it." Pam was in great shape. Dana smiled.

"Temptation," Pam growled, "thy name is Dr. Dana Perkins."

The phone rang. Afraid it was yet another parent, Dana rushed out of the office and left the building.

Chapter 10

Dana retrieved her car from home, drove to Shutter Lake Medical Clinic on the edge of town, then parked in the joint lot between the medical clinic and the Chamber of Commerce. The sprawling, one-story stucco-and-brick building sat nestled between towering trees that shimmered sunshine. She walked to the wide, welcoming porch with its broad rocking chairs and wondered if she shouldn't replace the chairs on her own front porch with rockers. She mentally added thinking about that to her to-do list and opened the tinted-glass door.

The medical clinic was as welcoming on the inside as on the outside. Comfortable cushioned chairs scattered in small groups created a charming lobby, and the magazines littering the tables were current issues, not cast-offs or ones a year out of date. From the council meetings, Dana knew the center was insanely well-equipped with the latest everything money could buy and technology could offer. That, Ana Perez had confided, was a fringe benefit in having an aging council accustomed to comfort and efficiency with gobs of money to spend. If they needed medical care, they wanted the best. Oddly, Ana didn't see herself as the center's best asset. Others did. But she did not.

"Dr. Dana Perkins," Ana came walking out of the hallway to her office, and let out an exaggerated gasp. "As I live and breathe."

Pam had called and told Ana that Dana was on her way. She smiled. "Call off the hounds. You won. I'm on my way to the lab right now."

"Well, just to make sure you don't disappear between here and there, I'll handle you myself. You've cost my staff a lot of time, trying to get you in here."

Dana had the grace to blush; her face heated. "Sorry."

"Mmm." Tall and thin with dark hair and eyes that twinkled amusement with her every word, Dr. Luciana Perez teased, but only someone empty-headed would believe she didn't mean every word she said.

"I apologize, and I'll remember not to trouble your staff unduly in the future."

"Great." She waved to a mother and young boy leaving the clinic. "No more swallowing pennies, Sam."

"I promise." The four-year-old boy lifted his right hand.

"Let's go to my office." Ana led the way through the hallway to her private domain.

"You painted it yellow."

"Last year." Ana grunted. "You really do have to stop dragging your physicals out, Dana."

She guessed she did.

"Grab a seat and I'll snag what I need to get your blood drawn."

Minutes later she was back and cuffing Dana's arm. "Your pressure is up. What's going on?"

"The students were wired for sound today," Dana said. "I expected it after that press conference yesterday."

"They weren't there."

"No." Dana slanted a glance at Ana. "But their parents were, and of course, whatever they say at home…"

"Comes right back to school through the kids." Ana removed the cuff.

"Exactly."

"How's the stomach?"

"It was a little better until today. The antacid is taking care of it, I think."

"Watch the spices."

"Definitely."

Ana drew two tubes of blood. "Not that you've asked, but everything looked great on your last physical. Test results all came back well within the normal range. You could do a little more Yoga and, I'm thinking, a little more meditation could help calm your stomach."

Dana groused but didn't comment. The smell of the alcohol wipe burned her nose. Talking with Thomas about Phoenix had upset her. So had pulling out the photo and crying half the night, but Vinn being in jail upset her just as much. "There's been a lot to deal with lately," Dana said. "For you also, with you and Sylvia being good friends. You okay?"

"It's kind of crazy," Ana admitted. "One minute I'm fine. The next, I'm crying, and the minute after, I catch myself dialing her phone number to share something with her."

"All of that is normal, Ana. It takes time."

"I know." She shrugged.

"Why didn't you ever invite her to our girls' night out?" Julia, Ana, Laney and Dana had been meeting on Wednesday nights for a long while now. Sylvia too was single. She would have fit right in.

Ana finished up and put a square of gauze on Dana's arm over the puncture wound then taped it into place. "I mentioned it to her once, but girls' night out is not really a Sylvia kind of thing." Ana shrugged. "She had lunch with the girls at her office every day. I guess that was enough for her."

Or maybe Ana wanted something separate of her own, like Sylvia's lunches. Something Sylvia and she didn't share. "Can I ask you a question?"

"Sure."

Dana rolled down her sleeve. "Did you ever treat any of the exchange students who stayed with the Windermeres?"

The used needle dropped to the bottom inside the red biohazard box. "You know I can't answer that."

Dana expected the medical privilege response and clarified. "No, I'm not asking for specifics. I was just reading about Venezuela. You know I went there a couple times before I moved to Shutter Lake."

"Of course. Your mask collection."

Dana nodded. "I was thinking about the student who was here for just a couple months. She worked part-time for Sylvia."

"Josie Rodriguez?" Ana disposed of the remaining blood-drawing remnants and sat down at her desk. "What about her?"

"Was she ill while she was here?"

"Not that I'm aware of."

"She left so suddenly." Dana buttoned her cuff. "Here one day, gone the next."

Ana's focus sharpened. "When I mentioned her at girls' night out last month, you told me Mrs. Windermere said there'd been a family emergency."

"That's what she told us at school regarding Josie's absence. Then, of course, a few days later, she let us know Josie wouldn't be coming back."

"So family emergencies don't come with advance notice. So what's wrong, Dana?"

No sense trying to hide it. Something in all that was troubling her. "Nothing," Dana said. When Ana just stared at her, Dana shrugged. "Okay, I'm not sure. Something…but probably nothing."

"What about it is the something?" Ana asked.

"It's just that I've never known an exchange student to give up their slot like that. They compete so hard to get it, you know? It just strikes me as odd."

"It did me, too."

"Really?" That got Dana's attention.

Ana nodded. "I didn't believe it. But I haven't found anything to contradict it."

Surprise shimmied through Dana. "You've looked."

"A little," Ana confided. "Okay, a lot. When a girl gets a break like that, to come here to school, she doesn't give it up without a fight. It's her one shot at a better life, and she knows it better than anyone else." Ana twisted her mouth. "So, yes, I've looked. Hard, actually. But I couldn't find anything."

Maybe Dana would have better luck. "One more question."

"Shoot, but make it quick. I've got a meeting with your favorite mayor."

Dana frowned. "Knock off the matchmaking, Ana. We're friends and colleagues. That's it."

"Uh-huh." She crossed her arms. "So what's your question."

"Did Sylvia tell you why she was going to Venezuela?"

"On vacation."

"That's what she's told everyone."

"And...?"

"I don't believe it." Dana had to make herself admit it aloud, but once she had, she knew she was right.

"Why not?"

"There's a travel advisory alert out. There's no food on the grocery-store shelves, and the government is a wreck. They're in real trouble. It's not a vacation paradise right now, that's for sure. So she had to have another reason for going."

"Sylvia was accustomed to her creature comforts." Ana thought long and hard. "But a vacation is all she told me. Except that she'd send me videos of her adventures."

"How could she do that?"

"Oh, she did videos all the time and emailed me the links to them. She has a private D.Tube channel."

"Have you looked to see if she sent you anything—"

"It's D.Tube, Dana. Not Heaven.com. No satellite transmissions from there to here."

Dana dipped her chin. "I meant from before she passed away."

"There aren't any. That, I checked," Ana confessed, sadness filling her eyes.

"Am I done?" She started to scoot off the chair.

"Yes—wait. It just hit me."

"What?"

"Josie. She was from—"

Their gazes locked, and Dana said, "Venezuela."

Ana drew in a sharp breath. "You think Sylvia was going there to find Josie?"

"I have no reason to think so," Dana admitted. "But I don't see why she'd take a vacation there right now, considering everything going on down there."

Ana darted her gaze from one side of the room to the other. "It'd be just like her to go retrieve Josie and march her back here—so she has her chance for a better life."

"That was my thought," Dana said. "She sure tried to help all her other employees improve their positions, and Josie is the only employee who ever left Sparkle, too, isn't she?"

Ana nodded. "So how do we find out if that's what Sylvia was doing?"

"We keep looking." Dana stood up. "Thanks for playing vampire."

Thoughtful, Ana nodded.

Dana walked down the hallway and in the lobby saw Thomas. "If Ana is late," she told him, "it's the council's fault."

He smiled. "Why is that, Dr. Perkins?"

"If they didn't require a full physical every year, she wouldn't have to draw blood from me, and she would have been on time for your meeting. So…"

"It's their fault. Got it." He shook his head. "But I'm glad they finally got you in to take care of it. Now Gracie will stop reminding me we don't yet have the report."

She sniffed. "Well, at least it's done. A terrible waste of good money—I'm fine—but it's done. So Gracie can quit telling Pam to nag me about doing it." She didn't mention Ana's staff's nagging also. "It's costing me some German Chocolate cupcakes."

"Really sorry." From his smile and the twinkle in his eye, he didn't look sorry at all. "You free for dinner?"

"I am, if we can make it an early night." She needed to look at Kristina's project. Vinn's had been revealing. Maybe hers would be, too. And she needed to dig a little more on Josie Rodriguez. If Ana's intuition was telling her something wasn't right there, then maybe something wasn't right, and Sylvia heading to Venezuela wasn't just a coincidence.

"How about we meet at Fitzgerald's at seven."

"That'd be wonderful. I've never been there for dinner."

"I know, and after the delicious meal you made for us last night and my abrupt departure, it's only right that I take you."

Dinner on the lake sounded soothing. "It sounds great. I'll see you there."

"Mayor Jessup?" Ana called out from a few steps away. "Are you here to see me?"

"Now, I'm in trouble for keeping the tyrant waiting."

"You know she is a stickler about her schedule," Dana whispered.

"She is." He winked. "See you tonight."

"Mayor?" Ana nudged him.

"Yes, Dr. Perez." He turned his attention to Ana. "Right here."

Dana smiled farewell to the receptionist, then checked her watch. She had ample time for a stop at Batter Up Bakery before meeting with Wade Travis—and he'd better come to her office armed with the truth...and with a willingness to tell it.

Chapter 11

Inside Batter Up Bakery, Dana spotted Laney seated at one of two small tables, munching her way through a cupcake with buttercream frosting. From the troubled look on her face, this wasn't going to be a quick stop, after all. "Drowning your sorrows?" she asked.

Laney looked over at her. "I'm fine."

The woman was anything but fine. Dark smudges under her eyes, tension in her jaw, and a haunted look all too familiar to Dana when looking in the mirror into her own eyes. Laney wasn't sleeping well, and she was drowning her sorrows in cupcakes. "You know if you need to talk, I'm here."

"I know. Everyone knows." Laney curved her lips in what should pass to the untrained as a smile. "You're the Shutter Lake keeper of secrets."

"The what?" Dana crooked her tote on her arm. "Who told you that?"

"No one. Everyone just knows it, Dana. Well, everyone except you, apparently." Laney shrugged. "Honestly, I guess it was a tossup between you and Sylvia Cole—you can't hide things from someone who goes through your things all the time—but since she's gone now…"

"I win the title by default." Interesting. Keeper of secrets. Dana had no idea people felt that way, much less talked about it to one another.

"I guess you do." Laney nodded. "No disrespect."

"No offense taken." Actually, there were a lot of worse things a person could be known for. Being able to keep secrets, especially around here, sounded pretty good. At times, it was a bigger burden to lug around others' secrets than to haul our own. But everybody needs someone safe to talk to about things. From her own experiences, she understood that better than most. Everyone has trials and challenges, and some secrets cut so deep and are so dark we don't want others to have a clue they exist in us. "So what's wrong?"

"Oh, you don't have to be polite with me, Dana. With all the upset going on, all the kids and their parents on edge, you don't need me dumping on you, too."

That cutting loose and letting go was the purpose of girls' night out. At least, it was for Dana. "I'm a psychologist, remember? I'm trained for it." Dana sat down and placed her handbag and tote on the floor at her feet. "Dump away."

"No, seriously. I'm okay."

"Laney, we're friends. If I can't be here for you when you clearly need me, that's a fail. Friends are there for friends, whenever they're needed. Now stop being the strong one who can handle everything —most of the time, you are—but right now, you need a friend. Let me be one, okay?"

"Okay." Laney chewed a bite of cupcake slowly and then swallowed. "You know I worked homicide in Los Angeles, right?"

Dana nodded. Now wasn't the time for her words. It was time for her ears—to listen.

"Do you know I left because I shot and killed a twelve-year-old boy?"

Pain ripped through Dana's chest. She hadn't known, and gave Laney a negative nod. With Laney, this might be a first, voluntarily saying those words out loud. Dana schooled her expression, careful it remain a non-judgmental mask.

"Well, I did." Laney's chin trembled. "It was dark and he had on this hoodie. I couldn't really see his face, just his silhouette. He'd already shot my partner, and I was chasing him. All of a sudden, he stops, turns and draws down on me. I'm looking down the barrel of his gun." She stopped, clearly reliving that moment in her mind.

Dana intruded. "It was shoot or be shot."

Laney nodded, lowering her gaze to the half-eaten cupcake. "When I saw he was a kid…" Her voice cracked. She took a sharp breath and let it out slowly. "I quit." She forced her gaze to Dana's. "I was cleared of any wrongdoing, but…I quit. And then I came here."

"For the peace and tranquility," Dana said in low hushed tones, just above a whisper.

"Exactly." Laney rubbed her thigh, as if drying a damp palm.

"And now, with Sylvia's murder, what happened then has followed you here and stirred up all those old memories."

"Yes."

"And you're having trouble coping?" Dana understood only too well. How could she not?

"Nightmares, Dana. Bad ones." Laney started to reach for her coffee, but her hand trembled so badly, she drew it back. "I keep reliving it."

"He's haunting your dreams?"

"He is." Laney shook it off, setting her long ponytail to sweeping across her shoulder. "I don't get it. He would have killed me."

"Yes."

"And it's not like I haven't regretted what happened. I have, a thousand times. I was cleared of wrongdoing, but in my dreams…"

Dana folded her hands atop the table. "You try to change the outcome. You look for other actions you could have taken, for anything—*anything*—different you could have done."

"Yeah." Laney seemed surprised.

"And yet the same thing happens over and over again, and because it does, the wound inside you keeps festering and stays raw."

Laney straightened and stopped rubbing her thigh. "You know exactly what it's like."

"Unfortunately, I do," Dana admitted. "Before I came to Shutter Lake, for peace and tranquility, I taught at an elementary school in Phoenix. There was a mass shooting. Long story short, I lost four students. When the shooting started, we weren't in our classroom, we were in a hallway, and there was nowhere to go. Finally, we ran back to a janitor's closet and piled into it. I sat closest to the door. It was hot and locked and the kids were so scared. I told them we had to be quiet and maybe the shooter wouldn't know we were there. He'd turned his back and started firing in another direction."

"So you saved the kids."

Dana let her agony show in her eyes. "Four died." She recited their names. "Cara, Misty, Sara and Joshua." She tugged at her earlobe and swallowed a lump of fresh tears from her throat. "Part of me died, too."

"Yes." Laney sparked recognition. "Exactly." She sipped from her coffee. "So you have nightmares, too."

"I did for more than five years. But this with Sylvia...it's brought them back."

"So they never end."

"Regret is merciless, Laney. That's the simple truth. But we get better at coping with it. And that, my friend, is also the truth."

"Merciless, I've got down pat. It's something...else, something that eases this stuff, I'm still searching for."

"Yes, I know." Dana tapped her folded forefingers. "We search because we feel guilty that we couldn't prevent the incident. Because we couldn't do more. Guilt tells us we're there to protect and defend, and when we fail, for whatever reason we fail, we might receive forgiveness from everyone else in the world, but we struggle —oh, how we struggle—to forgive ourselves."

Laney stilled and stared at Dana for a long time. "It's not regret, it's guilt that rises up again and torments us."

"It does, but guilt can't ease things in us any more than regret could, because it isn't what's really tormenting us," Dana said.

"Then what is?"

"Our lack of forgiving ourselves."

Laney winced. "I'm missing a step here."

Dana had, too. For a very long time. "Forgiveness is tricky. We think we forgive others so they can move forward, and so we do. But we don't accept that we must forgive ourselves so that we can move forward, too." Dana let that sink in. "It's really hard for us to admit, especially to ourselves, that we were helpless. Or that we tried and just plain failed. So we forgive everyone else, no problem. But we don't forgive ourselves because way down deep in places we don't talk about or even acknowledge exist, we have this spark of doubt. We hang onto it with all we've got, and we continue to believe there is something else we could have done. Some way we could have changed the outcome."

"Second-guessing ourselves, so it comes out in our dreams." Laney grunted. "I get it."

"Here's the most important part," Dana said. "Until we accept that what happened did happen and it's done, we're stuck on this hamster wheel of hell. There's only one thing that can stop the wheel so we can get off."

"What?"

"Us actually forgiving ourselves. That is the only act that can set us free. It's simple but complex and hard to do, yet once we do it, we're free to move on."

"You did that."

"I had done that," Dana corrected her. "Last summer, I went to Shutter Lake and had a picnic all by myself. It was a beautiful day. Warm, the sun felt so good. The sky for some reason seemed even more blue than usual, and I knew it was time to face my past head on." Dana dropped her voice even lower. "The school in Phoenix gave me an award for saving fourteen kids. I went to the lake that day to burn it because I lost four." Dana lifted her thumb and stared at it. "So I lit this lighter and, when the flame got close to the paper, it hit me."

"What?"

"In mourning the four and not forgiving myself, I was failing to show any gratitude at all that fourteen kids lived." Tears shimmered in Dana's eyes, blurring Laney's face. "That night, fourteen beautiful children went home and not to the morgue because I got them into that closet." Dana smiled. "Until that moment, I had never, not once, ever looked at what happened that way."

Laney smiled back. "You didn't burn the award."

"I framed it." Dana's voice came out stronger. "It's on the back of my bedroom door where I see it last thing at night and first thing every morning before going to school."

"Wow." Laney blinked, and her smile faded. "But you're having nightmares again."

"Just for a couple of nights." Dana shrugged. "The bad stuff is easier to remember and harder to forget than the forgiveness."

"Seems to always work that way."

"It does."

Laney took a bite of cupcake, mulled all that over. "So if I forgive myself, the nightmares should stop."

"Maybe," Dana said, not wanting to pass false hope. "You might still have some, but if you really forgive yourself, you'll have more strength and be better able to handle them. They won't cut as deep. You might get an acid stomach, but what happened and your part in it, won't eat your heart out like it has been. In your work there, think about the ones you helped spare, Laney."

"Makes sense." Laney nodded. "I'll give it a try."

"A tip from the trenches, friend to friend. Don't try. Do it."

"Total resolve."

"Definitely." Dana stood up, scooted her chair back under the table. "Total resolve."

"Thanks, Dana."

"Any time." She tilted her head. "We're survivors, but we're not alone. Everyone who has reached puberty is walking wounded from something."

"It helps to remember it." Laney smiled up at Dana. "You're a good psychologist."

"Thank you." Dana sniffed. "But I'm shooting for being better at protecting kids."

"After all that happened, I can see why you would be."

No better time to tick an item off her to-do list, Dana thought.

"When we were dealing with the DNA trash, I should have mentioned that Vinn and Kristina were more than friends. I got sidetracked, but I didn't forget it. I am sorry for the delay."

"It's okay, Dana. I'm sure it staying on your to-do list irritated you a lot more than me." Laney smiled. "I kind of thought there might be more between those two."

"Pretty innocent, I think," Dana said. "But speaking of Vinn, there is something—"

Laney's expression shuttered, but regret tinged it. "Dana, you know I can't talk about the case."

"Oh, of course, I do. I don't want to talk about the case." Laney's relief was immediate, so Dana went on. "I want to talk to Vinn."

"Why?"

She didn't dare reveal her thoughts. "I expect he could use a friendly eared psychologist right about now."

"I don't doubt it." Laney paused a second, then added, "I might be able to get McCabe to agree on those terms—you being Vinn's psychologist—if Vinn wants to see you."

Hope raised in Dana. She tried and failed to tamp it. "Let me know."

"I will. I'll talk to McCabe when I get back to the office."

"Wait until a little later in the afternoon," Dana whispered. "I hear he's more receptive then."

Shock pumped through Laney. "How do you—"

Dana pressed a fingertip over her lips. "All is well."

Laney nodded.

At the counter, Dana called out to Heidi and checked her watch. The emotionally charged conversation with Laney had seemed to last a lifetime, but time-wise, Dana was okay. "Heidi, are you back there?"

She popped her head through the door. "Been hiding out. You and Laney looked pretty intense over there and I didn't want to intrude."

"That was very thoughtful of you."

"Trying to make amends after yesterday, but they say Connie is doing okay today. I still can't believe I said that out loud."

"It happens." Dana brushed the faux pas aside. "I need two German Chocolate cupcakes."

"Ah, you're tempting Pam again. What'd she do this time?"

"Nagging," Dana confided.

"You do hate that."

"Yes, I do." Dana let out a little laugh.

"She means well. Pam's a good person."

"The best. Would I reward her with your cupcakes if she weren't?"

"Ha." Heidi beamed. "I guess not. " She reached for a small box and her tongs.

An item from Dana's to-do list sprang to mind. "I'd like to arrange something, if you are open to it."

"What's that, Dr. P.?"

Heidi had always called her Dr. P. From the first time they'd met. "Every Wednesday, Sylvie used to take Troy Duval a treat."

"A bagel. Blueberry, if it's available. He's fond of blueberries and they're great antioxidants, so they're particularly good for him." She dropped her voice so only Dana could hear. "He loves my butter cream frosting, too, but Sylvia won't bring it to him because he's supposed to watch his sugar."

Everyone in Shutter Lake loved Heidi's butter-cream frosting. "Can you continue that—a Wednesday treat for him—and bill me for it?"

That surprised her. "Well, I could if I made blueberry bagels, but I don't. You have to get them from The Grind." Heidi hooked a thumb next door.

"Oh, gee. I know that. I've stood in line with Sylvia a hundred times."

"No problem," Heidi said. "Nolan Ikard will probably do it. Tightwad will likely add a delivery fee."

"Sorry, Heidi, and thanks. I'll set it up with him then." Dana stretched out a bill to settle up.

"Wait. Why are you doing that?"

"Mr. Duval is ill and a shut-in. Since Sylvia died, I don't think he sees anyone except Renata Fernandez."

"I heard she's doing his house on Wednesdays. Sylvia always took care of him herself." Heidi leaned against the counter. "Renata's a sweet girl, but she's no Sylvia. She's scared to death of Troy Duval."

"Why on earth would she be afraid of him?" The man was a senior and frail. He posed no threat to anyone.

Heidi lifted a hand. "She's scared to death of everybody and everything." Heidi turned an assessing eye on Dana. "So why are you getting involved?"

Why was she? Maybe because she was alone in the world, too. Maybe because she hoped that one day someone remembered she was alone and let her know she hadn't been forgotten. "Because I can."

That set Heidi back on her heels. "I'll tell you what, Dr. P. It'll be hard—Nolan and I don't exactly get along—but I'll get the bagel from The Grind and drive it out to Troy Duval for a while. Maybe we can set up a monthly rotation with some of the gals from church or something. Get some more people out there to see him."

"Thank you, Heidi." Considering she and Nolan Ikard had been at war ever since Dana had moved to the lake, this was a big concession on Heidi's part. "That's a great idea."

"I'll take it on and set it up. Consider it done."

"Wonderful." Happy inside. It felt good. "You just bill me then."

"For the bagel. Delivery is on me," Heidi said, adjusting her chef's hat. "No way is a penny of my money going to Nolan Ikard."

"Well, it's very good of you to do this. I appreciate it."

"It's nothing." Heidi waved off the praise. "If I were good, I'd have trotted myself out there to see about him a long time ago. But after yesterday, I'm going to try to be better."

Blurting out that comment about Vinn had kept Heidi up last night, too. "Being better is a great example. We all need to try harder."

"I guess." Heidi wiped off the counter. "Shame it takes losing one of our own to treat those left a little kindlier, but…"

"Never kick a silver lining to the curb, I say." Dana picked up the pink-striped box of two German Chocolate cupcakes and headed to the door.

If she hurried, she'd make the meeting with Wade Travis without being late. He'd been so edgy about it, it wouldn't surprise her a bit if he seized a one-minute delay as a justifiable reason to bolt.

Certain of it, she rushed her steps.

Chapter 12

For the most part, the students had left the school grounds. Small groups stood clustered chatting with friends, but the buses had departed and Dana had passed the bulk of the walkers about a block down the street.

She climbed the steps then But entered the building, nodding at a couple of basketball players heading to the gym for practice. Oh, how she wished Vinn were with them. He had to be scared to death, even in a small jail like McCabe's.

In the outer office, Wade Travis sat waiting on the far end of the row of four chairs. Pam heard Dana enter and looked up. "Ah, there you are, Dr. Perkins. Mr. Travis is here."

Dana glanced over at him. His skin looked gray, his expression solemn. His white shirt, black sweater and slacks just made him look more ashen. The worst was, his hands were shaking…and empty. "Mr. Travis, are you ill?"

"I'm fine, Dr. Perkins."

He wasn't fine. He had dreaded this coming conversation all day and seemed to be unraveling right before her eyes. Why?

Kristina Sharapova stepped into the office. "Dr. Perkins, I need to talk to you."

She seemed excited, eager to share something she deemed important. That was obvious. "Of course, Kristina. Wait in my office, please." Dana paused until she was seated inside her office, then pivoted to look at Travis. "Why don't you grab your laptop? This with Kristina will only take a minute."

He stared at her as if struck dumb. "Why?"

"It's school-issue. I need to see it. Now, please." The best way to get the information she needed to help him quickly was to see where he was before the murder and compare it to where he is now. His lesson plans and correspondence with students would show her that faster than he could tell her. He was troubled and needed assistance now.

Flustered, he gained his feet and left the office.

"He isn't himself." Pam asked, worry and curiosity burning in her eyes. "School issue?"

Likely she was curious. Rarely before had Dana inspected any teacher's laptop. But rarely had there been a need. "The laptop is school-issue, and we do have the right to inspect them at any time without notice. I need unfiltered information fast if I'm to help him," Dana said. "I want you to access Mr. Travis's laptop right now and let me know if you see anything on it I need to know about. Do it quickly, Pam."

"Before he can delete anything?" She swiveled to her keyboard. "I'm on it."

Why would he delete anything? Dana hadn't even considered... He had better not dare to delete anything. But if he tried... "Create a mirror of his hard-drive and note the time." That would be faster and give them an exact image before he could get back to his class-room and log in.

"Covered. Already there and in progress." She frowned. "What am I looking for?"

"Start in any personal files," Dana said, shifting her thinking. When she'd told him to get the laptop, Travis had reacted strongly. His face had bleached. There was something on it he didn't want her to see. No sense in speculating on what it was; she would know soon enough. Inside, she cringed at what that might be, but she would do what must be done. Protecting the kids. They always came first. Protecting her staff. Also extremely important.

"All right."

"Thanks." Dana didn't have time to mince words or to reassure her. Having an efficient assistant was reason enough to be grateful. But having one who trusted you enough to do what you asked without a ton of questions was a divine gift.

Dana entered her office and closed the door. "So, Kristina, what can I do for you?"

She rocked on the edge of her seat. "I remembered something."

No eye contact. It wasn't a comfortable memory, that much was clear. "Okay." Dana slid onto her chair behind her desk.

Kristina stood up. "I shouldn't sit. Mrs. Windermere is waiting for me. We're going shoe shopping."

"Sounds like fun." She'd get there. Hopefully sooner rather than later. "So what did you remember?"

"That night… The one when Sylvia Cole was murdered." Kristina paused and waited for Dana's acknowledgment, then went on. "Vinn and I met down the street from her house. I already told the police that, but I remembered I hadn't told you. We didn't do anything wrong. Vinn and me, I mean. We just talked. But he was there with me, Dr. Perkins."

The time of death was narrowed to three hours, from nine to midnight. "How long was he there with you?"

"That's not important."

"It could be, if you are saying he couldn't have killed Sylvia because you were together."

"I know he didn't kill Sylvia. Because of what I remembered."

Dana honed her focus. "What did you remember?"

"I was walking to meet Vinn, and this man ran out of Sylvia's backyard and down the street past me. He didn't see me or anything. I was under the trees and it's really dark out there at night."

"A man."

She nodded enthusiastically. "He wasn't Vinn. He was…

someone else. I don't know who, but he wasn't Vinn and he was running really, really fast."

"And the police know this?"

Again, she nodded.

"And you're sure—absolutely sure—he wasn't Vinn?"

"Positive." She shoved her backpack up on her shoulder by its sling strap. "Seeing that man running like that scared me, so I hurried up to the end of the street. Vinn was there waiting for me. He couldn't have gotten there, Dr. Perkins. Not when the guy had been running the other way. He wasn't Vinn."

"So you think this man could be the man who killed Sylvia."

"He was running out of her backyard really, really fast. Cutting through parked cars and everything."

Dana worried her jaw. "So why is Vinn claiming it was him?"

"I don't know," Kristina said in a flat tone rife with irritation. "He was seriously angry back then. I mean seriously angry."

"About what?"

"He never would say. I promise." Kristina said. "But I think it might have had to do with his parents."

"His parents?" Connie and Vernon might have the usual problems couples do, but they had to have it together to raise a kid like Vinn. That kind of rearing didn't happen by accident. Vinn was a mama's boy and everyone knew it. He adored her. What could Connie Bradshaw do to anger her son enough for it to last for weeks? Dana couldn't imagine. But his father... Boys Vinn's age always tested their fathers. Trapped between being a boy and a man, they pushed the boundaries, trying to find themselves and where they fit. It was a rite of passage thing. That seemed far more likely.

"I think probably he was mad at his dad," Kristina said. "I can't see Vinn getting and staying mad at his mom."

"Me, either." Dana looked over at Kristina. "But what would he be that mad at his dad about?"

"I asked, but he wouldn't tell me. He said he would never talk about it. Not if he lived to be a thousand. It had to be really bad."

Something in her tone set off a warning in Dana. "Why do you say so, Kristina?"

"Because I watched Vinn when the two of them talked. He looked at his dad like he hated him. It was so strong, Dr. Perkins. I've never seen Vinn do that before. He wasn't just mad at his dad. Right then, he hated him."

"And how did he look at his mother?"

"He was sad. Really sad. The kind of sad you feel when somebody you love dies." She cocked her head. "You know, when it hurts so bad you can't even tell where the pain starts or stops. It just hurts. That's all you feel."

The situation with his parents had to be the source of Vinn's trouble at the time. This, for Vinn, wasn't about something his father had done to him. It was about something his father had done that had hurt his mother.

Dana smiled at Kristina. "Thank you for sharing that with me. I really appreciate it, and I think it might just help."

"Really?" Her face brightened.

"Really."

"You will try to help Vinn, won't you, Dr. Perkins?"

"You know I will." She winked to confirm her promise.

And it was a promise Dana intended to keep.

Chapter 13

BREAKDOWN

Wade Travis and Kristina crossed paths, leaving and entering Dana's office.

He'd just settled into the chair, clutching the laptop, when Pam stepped in. "Sorry to interrupt, Mr. Travis." She pivoted her gaze to Dana. "Dr. Perkins, I need a moment, please."

Pam had that look in her eye, and Dana's stomach clenched. She'd found something in his personal files. "Excuse me a second, Mr. Travis."

He didn't respond.

Dana stepped out, and Pam shut the door to ensure their privacy. "You're not going to like this," Pam said, dropping her voice to a whisper. "I feel like I need to bleach my eyeballs."

"What is it?"

"Porn. Lots and lots of porn."

The fool had put porn on his school laptop. Dana's heart rocketed and sank. "Students?"

"No, thank God. Grown women, but...very explicit." Pam visibly shuddered.

Dana closed her eyes, steeled herself. "Okay. Okay, not a word to anyone."

Pam nodded then returned to her desk, her legs a little wobbly.

That told Dana more than her assistant's words. Pam didn't wobble easily. But this had shaken her. With a deep breath, Dana turned the knob and opened the door, then stepped back into her office, closing the door softly behind her.

Without a word, she extended her hand for the laptop. When Mr. Travis passed it to her, she fought the feeling of holding slime. "When I look at the files on this piece of school property, what am I going to find, Mr. Travis?"

He slumped and the blood drained from his face. "Oh, God."

Dana's jaw clamped tight. "I sincerely doubt God has anything to do with this."

He regrouped and let out a cackle. "It's nothing, Dr. Perkins."

That infuriated her. When she thought she had control of her voice, she set the laptop down on the credenza behind her desk. "Oh, I disagree," she said. "This is something. You're a teacher at *my* school, interacting with *my* students, Mr. Travis. That makes this nothing a *big* something."

"You know." The caginess in his eyes dimmed and went flat.

"I know."

He lifted a hand. "I have never touched a kid in my life. I swear it. Never. That's vile and disgusting." He caught himself and lowered his elevated voice. "I love my students, Dr. Perkins. I would never—"

"Save it," Dana interrupted. "Why do you do it? You know what you're risking."

"It's an addiction," he said without regret. "It's vile and disgusting to me, so I can imagine how it seems to you. I swear every time I'm going to quit. It's the last time. But...it never is." He dragged a shaky hand over his bald pate. "I don't know why."

A puzzle piece clicked into place in Dana's mind. "Sylvia Cole knew."

"What?" He drew back, growled. "No."

Dana didn't believe him. "Yes. Sylvia knew and that's why you've been so upset since her murder."

No answer.

Dana glared at him in total silence.

Finally, he broke. "Okay, she knew." He shook his head, "We were supposed to meet the night she was killed. But she didn't show up."

"You've told the police this, I assume?"

"No."

"Why not?"

He darted his gaze across the ceiling. "I was afraid to tell them anything."

He hadn't wanted anyone to know. Dana could certainly understand that. The man Kristina had seen running from Sylvia's backyard. "So you went to her house and killed her to keep your secret."

"I did not. I swear it." He wagged a finger at her. "But that's exactly why I didn't tell anyone we were supposed to meet that night. I knew I'd be blamed for killing her, and I didn't do it." He planted his feet on the floor, pulled a man-spread and propped his hands on his knees. "I did not kill that woman, okay? She did find out about my addiction. And I did pay her to stay quiet about it. But I did not kill her."

Secrets. Everyone had secrets. "So Sylvia was blackmailing you."

"Yes!" Mr. Travis realized he'd shouted and schooled himself. "She called it buying her cooperative assistance. It was blackmail," he said. "I paid her to keep my addiction to herself. But I swear I did not kill her."

Dana frowned. "Was she blackmailing anyone else?"

"How would I know? Who'd want to know?" He shrugged. "That's not the kind of thing you ask or go around talking about."

True. Dana worried her inner cheek. "Tell me about Venezuela."

He squirmed.

"I'm not asking for fun, Mr. Travis. You can tell me or I call Chief McCabe and you can tell him. Right now."

He squeezed his eyes shut, and when he reopened them, resignation burned in their depths. "I knew she was going, okay?"

"Why did she tell you?"

His frown and resignation slid deeper, lining his face with long creases from the sides of his nose down to his mouth. "Because I'm the reason she was going."

"Excuse me?"

He was extremely embarrassed and deeply annoyed. "Sylvia found the porn on my computer at home and confronted me. We argued."

"Sylvia did your house herself?"

"Josie usually cleaned for me. But when she left so fast, Sylvia filled in, until she could fit me into one of the other girl's schedules."

Josie did his house. "So how does that tie to Venezuela?"

"I told you. We argued. Sylvia wanted more money. I refused. I told her I shouldn't have to pay more when she could just get another girl from one of the porn sites like she had Josie."

"What?" Genuinely shocked, Dana leaned forward on her desk.

"I saw her," he said. "Well, I saw a girl on one of my favorite sites that could have been her. I'm not a hundred percent sure she was Josie. But they kind of favored. Anyway, Sylvia went a little crazy about it and started screaming threats at me. I told her if she said one word about my addiction to anyone, I'd tell everyone on the lake she was running porn stars through Sparkle."

"You saw Josie on one of your favorite sites?" Dana's mind whirled, refusing to wrap around this.

"I told you, I'm not a hundred percent sure it was her. But the girl favored her. I saw her more than once, but I'm still not sure."

"How many times did you see her, Mr. Travis?"

"Five. Maybe a few more. Sylvia made me show her."

"Did you?"

"No choice." He nodded. "Sylvia wasn't sure either, but she still went ballistic."

Dana processed all that. "So how did Quentin and Kathleen Windermere get involved in this and maybe end up with a porn star as an exchange student?"

"I don't know that they did. It might not have been her, and it seems unlikely the Windermere's would be involved in something like that."

"Yet Sylvia was going to Venezuela."

"She wasn't sure either," Travis said. "But you know how protective Sylvia was about the people working for her. She swore that night she was going to find out and, if she was Josie, to get her back." He rotated his shoulders. "I tried to tell Sylvia that the site was Viva Venezuela, but that didn't mean anything."

"What should it mean?" Dana had not a clue.

"They move all the time." He lifted his hands. "Who knows where that girl is really?"

Maybe or maybe not actually in Venezuela. "What's her...stage name?"

"Vivian. Viva Vivian." He didn't meet Dana's eyes.

She jotted the site and stage name down on her Things to Tell Laney list.

"How did an exchange student going home on a family emergency end up in a porn film?" Dana said out loud.

"I don't know that she did. But if she did, she probably got there the same way most do. Someone groomed her for it or snatched her and threw her into it." He lost his animation and added, "Sylvia said if Josie had ended up a victim of human trafficking, she was going to kill the bastard responsible." He flushed. "Sorry for the language, Dr. Perkins, but that's what she said."

"You had nothing to do with that transition, then?"

"No way. I watch. That's it." He raised his right hand. "I really don't know if the girl was Josie, but a lot of women from her hometown do end up trafficked. She told me that herself once."

What was he doing, having a conversation like that with Josie? "That woman was sixteen years old," Dana reminded him.

"I didn't know that when we had the conversation. I thought she was eighteen. And I thought it when I saw her on the site, too. I check for that. I don't want anything to do with underage kids."

"The trafficker lied." And Sylvia might have been unsure Viva Vivian was Josie, but it looked as if she was determined to try to find out.

"I—I didn't know it." Travis's eyes stretched wide. "I warned Sylvia against messing with those kind of people."

He thought a trafficker had killed her. "Why didn't she just call Josie's family?"

"She did. But the number had been disconnected. She called the local police there, too. The family had moved."

"Where to?"

"I don't know. Sylvia didn't say."

"So was she still going on her trip?"

"I don't know that either," he admitted. "If she'd showed up that night, she might have told me, but she didn't. Next thing I heard, she was dead."

Dana shifted focus and pounded him with questions about the students for a solid hour. Finally, she felt satisfied he hadn't compromised them, so she gave him a choice. "You can go to Dr. Perez and check yourself into the clinic for addiction treatment, or I'll phone Chief McCabe and report all this right now. Your call."

"No." His eyes stretched. "I've told you everything, I swear. You do this, and I'll lose my job. You can't do this to me."

"I'm not doing anything to you, Mr. Travis. You've done it to yourself. " Dana stiffened. "Your job is gone. I can't have you around the students. That is not going to happen."

"But teaching is all I've got."

It was, and he was good at it. But this…this was a bridge too far. He'd crossed it on his own. Now he had to live with the consequences of his actions. "You gave me no choice. My first responsibility is to the children." She reached for the phone and pushed it toward him. "Make your decision, Mr. Travis."

"If I go for rehab, afterward can I come back to teach?"

"No. I'm sorry. I can't have teachers I can't trust around my students. But the personal benefits to you of rehab should be self-evident."

He let that sink in, then started to rise.

"Sit down." She barked the order.

"I'm going to the clinic."

"Stay in that chair. Don't move again or I'll have security restrain you. I don't want to humiliate you, Mr. Travis, but I will."

He sat back down but, not trusting him, Dana felt for the phone and dialed, maintaining eye contact the whole time.

"Shutter Lake Medical Clinic."

"Dr. Perez, please. Tell her it's Dr. Perkins." Oh, but Dana hoped Ana was available.

A long two minutes later, Ana came on the line. "What's wrong, Dana? Is it your stomach?"

"No. I need you to pick up Wade Travis as soon as possible. He's in my office waiting for you."

"What for? Is he injured?"

"No, he isn't injured." Dana regretted the indignity of this conversation but it couldn't be helped. "He has a porn addiction and needs treatment immediately."

"That's not typically an addiction we treat in-patient."

"Let me be clear, Dr. Perez." Dana forced her tone formal. "He'll be an in-patient or I'll call Chief McCabe to take Wade Travis to jail." The object of the discussion flinched. "Those are his options. My students will not have to worry about this, too."

"I understand." Ana's breath hissed through the phone. "Is he agreeable or hostile?"

"He is agreeable to in-patient treatment." If he disputed her, she'd call McCabe and that would be that.

"I'll send an ambulance over for him right away."

"Thank you. He'll be sequestered in my office until they arrive to retrieve him." Mr. Travis looked beaten down. She didn't want to feel sympathetic toward him, but it flickered through her anyway. "Dr. Perez, keep him on a very tight leash."

"I need a minute. Give me just a second." Ana put her on hold. When she returned, she said, "Ten minutes."

"Great."

"I can't expect he's too happy with you right now. Are you safe?"

"I'm fine."

"They've been dispatched," Ana said. "Don't let him get between you and the office door, and do not turn your back on him. Think caged animal."

"I won't."

"When are they coming?" Travis asked.

"They're already on the way," Dana said. "Thanks, Dr. Perez."

"I'd feel better if you'd stay on the phone with me until they arrive." Ana spoke to someone in her own office. "Tell them to move it!"

"It's not an issue," Dana assured her. "Thank you." She hung up the phone.

Travis was shaking all over. "You know, now she knows, and you're going to tell the council. By tomorrow everyone on the lake will know."

Humiliation was always a bitter pill to swallow. Life as Wade Travis had known it was over. "I have no choice, Mr. Travis. You know that. There are protocols."

"Forget your protocols. This is my life." Anger flinted through his eyes. "Some secrets are meant to be kept."

"Not when they impact my students and my school." The granite edge in her tone chilled him. "What did you expect would happen? You had to have thought about it. You had to know that one day you'd get caught."

"I did get caught. And I paid a boat-load of money to make the problem go away."

"Sylvia." Dana felt her temper hover the stratosphere. "I'm not Sylvia, and you're not sweeping this under any rug. You want to forget something, forget that." She forced her temper to cool, afraid it would be the tinder that would knock him over the edge and into violence. "I am sorry, Mr. Travis. You have an addiction. While I am sympathetic to that, I will not—I cannot—let sympathy supersede my duty to the students."

Pam opened the door without knocking. She'd been watching through the glass, standing back so Mr. Travis couldn't see her. The armed school resource officer stood beside her. "Sorry to interrupt," she said, sounding amazingly normal. "Two orderlies are here with the ambulance, they say, to retrieve Mr. Travis."

He stood up. "You ruined my life, Dr. Perkins. I hope you're happy."

"You ruined your life, Mr. Travis." Dana stood up. "And, no, I

SO MANY SECRETS

am not happy. This situation was needless and is tragic. As bitter and angry as you are, I promise you you're happier than you would have been if you ever had touched one of my students. So count your blessings."

One of the orderlies, a man well over six feet tall, came into Dana's office. "Let's go."

Wade Travis walked out and got into the ambulance.

And Dana took her first full breath since he had walked into her office.

"You okay?" Pam asked.

Dana nodded. "I will be, after I talk to the Council."

Pam groaned. "And the parents?"

"Them, too." Shutter Lake was up to its rafters in secrets. While Dana wished this whole sordid mess could be one of them, it couldn't. She had to know Wade Travis had been honest with her about the students. If he had behaved inappropriately toward one of them. Just one…

"Should I get Mayor Jessup on the phone?"

Dana checked her watch. After six. "No, I'm meeting him at seven. We'll talk then." She had to call Laney, and then alert the council. "Afterwards we'll deal with the parents."

"I'll draft a note to them and text it to you."

"That would be wonderful, Pam."

Chapter 14

"Thank you for dinner, Thomas." At his side, Dana walked down the wooden dock back to shore.

"You ate like a bird." He glanced out over the sun-spangled water. "Still upset over Wade Travis?"

"Yes." She didn't bother to lie. Thomas had been upset, too, but fortunately he had found no fault with the way she'd handled the issue thus far. "Thanks for notifying the council."

"Just following protocol." They reached the earthen bank of Shutter Lake, and he motioned toward a bench. "Shall we sit a while?"

"I'd like that." She veered to the bench and then sat down. Sunset wouldn't be for another forty minutes or so. It'd be soothing to see it tonight.

"Are you okay with their suggestions?" Thomas sat down beside her. The green in his tie was the same shade as his eyes.

"I think speaking to the parents of Travis's students and them speaking to their children themselves is the best way to go about it. Easier on the kids, and the parents choose how much to say. It really should be their call."

"I agree. Usurping parental rights is not what we want in this."

He looked up at the sky, watched a bird fly by. "When will they be notified?"

"Tonight." Dana smoothed her black sheath skirt. "Hopefully, that will avoid criticism for any delay."

"Dana, I hardly think they can complain about being notified within hours." He covered her hand with his. "Every parent in the lake knows how protective you are of the kids."

She hoped so. "I'll speak to any who ask, of course, but I'm praying hard none of the students relay any improprieties." Her face went hot. She'd handle it, but oh, it would be difficult.

"I know the council wasn't exactly enthused about you reporting it to the police, but I'm glad you took the decision out of their hands. It was the right thing to do."

"I'm legally obligated to report it to the police, and I thought the council might want to keep it private, which is why I phoned in the report on the way out here."

"Hard with Zion Cole being on the council."

Hard to discover your murdered daughter was blackmailing someone. Dana kept her thoughts on that to herself.

"McCabe?"

"No, he was out. Laney took the information," Dana said. "She's probably at the medical clinic talking with Travis right now."

Thomas stretched his arms out across the back of the bench. "You don't think Travis killed Sylvia, do you?"

It was a question, but it didn't really sound like one. More like he wanted confirmation on what he already knew. Dana gave it to him. "I don't think so. But I'm certain Vinn didn't."

Deep relief washed over Thomas's face. "Thank God."

"What?" Dana asked, a little taken aback at his relief. The lines of tension nearly disappeared from his face. "Thomas?"

He avoided her eyes. "I'm glad. Vinn...he's a good kid."

Definitely more than your garden variety relief. And now avoidance, pure and simple. Suspicion confirmed. Something here was very personal. "I never would have taken Sylvia for a blackmailer," Dana said.

"Well, she was."

She pivoted on the bench to look at him. "Spoken with the authority of one who knows, and without doubt."

No answer. Thomas didn't spare her so much as a glance, which troubled her.

"About Vinn," she said, turning the subject.

He did look at her then, stared for a long moment.

"Thomas, don't be shocked." Dana let the hint of a smile curve her lips. "I'm fond of you, and have been for a long time, and I've seen Vinn at school every day for seven years. Did you really think I'd never noticed how much like you he is?"

"What does that mean?"

"It means he looks like you, he acts like you, even shares a lot of the same body language."

"So you think he's my son." His jaw tightened, and he looked away.

"I have no idea," she answered honestly. "But from your reaction, I'd say you think he is."

Thomas let the silence between them stretch and yawn. Finally, he whispered, "Maybe."

He didn't know. "Connie Bradshaw was your teacher."

He nodded. "Senior year. She married Vernon and had Vinn right away."

Painful ghosts lurked in those words. Instinct and years of experience warned Dana to tread carefully. "You've thought all along that Vinn might be your son." A thought struck her. "Sylvia did, too." He would speak with authority if Sylvia had been blackmailing him and Travis.

"I didn't know. I still don't know for sure," Thomas admitted. "Back then, I didn't want to know. She was married to Vernon, I was on my way to college. We both had different plans for our lives, and we made different choices."

"You never talked about it?" How could they never talk about it?

"No, we never did." He paused, studied the water, then added, "Thought about it, but by the time I realized she was expecting, she was already married to Vernon. There was nothing to talk about then."

If she was married to another man, Dana guessed any window of opportunity for discussions Connie had firmly shut. "So neither of you ever acknowledged the possibility, years went by and then Sylvia found out and blackmailed you."

"That's pretty much it." He shrugged. "But I didn't kill her, Dana."

"I know." She did know. Thomas Jessup would never tarnish his image or Shutter Lake's image deliberately. He would leave first.

"Vinn is a good kid. He's happy most of the time. Or he was, until all this happened."

She clasped her hands together. "You've watched him."

"I have." Thomas nodded, dipped his chin. "I've never said anything to him, of course. I wouldn't do that. Connie and Vernon are his parents. They seem happy together, and they clearly love Vinn." Thomas rubbed at his chin, thinking. "But he's in trouble now, and I have to say, it bothered me that Vernon didn't even go into the police station when Connie lost it at the press conference. He stayed outside until Laney called him to come in."

While Vinn screamed for McCabe to get his mother out of there, and she screamed to see her son. Recalling it gave Dana chills. Both she and Julia Ford had noticed Vernon's staying outside and had thought it odd. "People often react to stress in strange ways, Thomas. It's their body's way of protecting itself."

"His wife needed him."

"But you were in there with them. Why?"

"They needed…"

"You?"

He shrugged.

"And because you might be Vinn's birth father…maybe, you felt you needed to step up?" Did he even know why he did it?

"Someone needed to. Vernon was like a zombie out there."

"I see."

"You know when I ran into you at Dr. Perez's office?"

She nodded.

"My meeting was to ask her about taking over Sylvia's duties with the chamber. But I also talked with her about DNA. Vinn's DNA I have. Mine, I didn't."

"So she's running the test, to see if you're his father."

He nodded. "We'll have the results back in a day or so."

"And then you'll decide."

"Decide what?" He swept a strand of hair back from her face with a gentle hand.

"Whether to destroy the little left in Vinn's life or to keep quiet and put him first."

Thomas drew back, stiffened. "What are you saying?"

Dana placed a hand on his sleeve. "I'm saying Vinn has a mom and dad and, until this with Sylvia, he's been happy and well-adjusted. They're a family, Thomas. Now he's lost everything except his family and you—who have never been more than the mayor to him—are thinking about telling him you're his father." She frowned. "Isn't that just a little selfish?"

He stood up, strode a short path in front of the bench, then back to her. Stuffing a hand into his slacks' pocket, he waited for two bikers to get out of earshot on the trail behind them running parallel to the lake. "I didn't see it that way. I saw him as abandoned, and I wanted him to know he wasn't alone."

That redeemed Thomas in Dana's eyes, except for one problem. "He isn't abandoned or alone. Vernon and Connie go to the station to see Vinn every day. And tomorrow," she said, sharing the news she had gotten only hours ago from Laney, "so am I."

"How are you seeing him?" Thomas seemed happy but also confused. "McCabe refused."

"He refused the principal," Dana said. "Tomorrow, I'm going in as Vinn's psychologist."

"Oh, wow." He stilled. "You're protecting him. You think Vinn is innocent and you're going to get him to tell you the truth to prove it."

"I'm going to try," she said. "I can't do it alone, and I'm not sure he will help me. I'm hoping he will. I am certain he's innocent." She let her gaze drift. "But I'm also certain he's covering for someone else, and that someone has a powerful, powerful hold over him."

"Who?" Thomas sat back down on the bench.

"I don't know." She had been honest, as far as she'd gone. Her speculations were not facts. "But I am going to do my best to protect him from that person and from himself." A cool breeze kicked up, chilling her. "The only thing that will help is the truth."

"Thank you for this. I won't forget it."

"He's my student, Thomas." She would protect her students or die trying.

"So what you're telling me is, whether or not I'm his birth father, Vinn doesn't need me. He needs his family. That is what you're saying, right?"

"I'm saying he needs his dad and his mom. The parents he knows and loves who know and love him."

"You're not going to tell Vinn about any of this." Thomas looked deep into her eyes. "I mean, we don't know, but either way, you're not going to tell him."

"I am not."

"You don't think I should either."

"Typically, I wouldn't share my opinion. But since you asked, no. No, I don't think you should tell him." She stayed serious, shifted perspective. "Put yourself in Vinn's position. In his eyes, his world is in shambles. We don't know why, and he might or might not know why. He thinks he does, which means he needs something to hold on to right now. Something he knows and that is comfortable. He doesn't need his mother's reputation trashed for her having an affair with one of her students. Vinn doesn't need to know his mayor might or might not be his dad. And he really doesn't need to know his father thought Vinn was his own son and now neither of them is sure whose he is, or what role they play in each other's lives."

"Whoa." Thomas collapsed back, studied the deep water and its murky depths. "So I need to mind my own business and stay out of their family's business—either way."

"That's my two cents." She patted his hand. "Some secrets are meant to be kept."

He grunted. "I guess that's the price we pay for not stepping up at the time we create them."

Maybe it was. Looked that way to her. Vinn had to come first. "Yeah, I guess so."

"I don't think I want to know the test results."

"Yes, you do." Dana sat back, stretched out her legs and crossed them at her ankles. "Because until you know for sure, you don't know how to feel about these things. And until you know how to feel, you can't let go. You're stuck in the past." She looked at him, feeling tender. "I get it now."

"Get what?"

"Why you've never married." She thought it through. "That's always puzzled me, I have to say. You're the image perfectionist. It was a breach that you weren't married with a couple of kids. But this explains why you never let a woman get close enough to snag your heart. You never let go, so in your heart, you're already married to the mother of your maybe son."

"I did the wrong thing back then. I should have spoken to Connie about it, but I didn't."

"Thomas, are you still in love with Connie?"

He shrugged. "Do you ever forget your first love?"

"No, but you do put them in the past where they belong. In your circumstances, I can see why you haven't, but you were a kid and you made a mistake. You don't need to pay for it for the rest of your life."

"Maybe I don't deserve a family, Dana. If Vinn is mine, I walked away."

"Actually, I think you said you went to school one day and Connie was gone. Then you heard she was married, and then you saw her and she was pregnant. That's not exactly walking away. She made all the decisions for both of you."

"I never asked."

"She was another man's wife."

"What's your point?"

"My point is, stop waiting for her. Stop punishing yourself. Just stop, and go on and live your life."

An older couple moved down the path, arm in arm. Dana and Thomas spoke briefly to them and they then walked on. The sun burned low, bright orange. Another few minutes and they'd see the sunset.

"I don't envy your having to deal with the parents on this Travis issue."

He'd had enough of burrowing into his past for now. So had she, not that Travis was an enjoyable topic. "I hate that this incident is going to shake their confidence in me, but I know it will."

"Why should it?"

"In their eyes, he works for me."

Thomas frowned. "How long did you know before firing him?"

"Three, maybe four—"

"Days or weeks?" he cut in.

"Minutes," she corrected him. "Not one second of which was he out of my sight or did he interact with any of my students."

"Were there any missed signs, warning you?"

"Before Sylvia's death, no. He's been upset ever since then, but so has everyone else." She cleared her throat. "I thought it was all the focus challenges or something. Turns out, he was afraid that her death would trigger the release of her blackmail fodder."

Thomas stiffened. "I never considered that."

"If it were going to happen, surely it would have already."

"So how did you find out about Travis?"

"I exercised a policy never before used and had Pam access his school-issued laptop for personal files. It was in his viewing history."

"But no files on his computer."

"No."

"So Pam compiled the information and you didn't see it?"

"I haven't seen it yet," Dana said. "I'll have to see it today in case he sues to keep his job."

"He wouldn't dare." Thomas's stern expression knit the skin between his eyes.

"I don't think so either."

"Spare yourself then."

"I can't."

"Why not?"

She wouldn't do it. She wouldn't tell Thomas Wade's suspicion that one of her students might have been trafficked. "According to Wade, those sites come and go quickly. We need proof of what is there now."

"I'm sorry, Dana."

"Me, too." She sighed. "He was a good history teacher."

Her phone signaled an incoming message. "I should get that. Could be Pam sending me the draft of our email to the parents."

He nodded. "Of course."

She pulled out her phone and checked the message. It was a text from Laney. *Vinn's parents agreed. Lawyer has signed off for you to speak with him. 6:30 tomorrow morning.*

Dana messaged back: *Be there.* Six-thirty was a lot earlier than she'd intended, but after the marathon she'd had to run to gain permission to talk with Vinn, she'd be willing to go in at midnight. She dropped her phone back into her purse. "Sorry about that."

"No problem." His expression sobered. "I just hope we don't end up neck-deep in lawsuits by any parents. "Are you sure there's been no inappropriate behavior with the kids?"

Asking the question embarrassed Thomas deeply. Considering his own history with Connie, Dana understood that. "Travis said there wasn't, and he seemed sincere. We've had no complaints, and Pam said the sites he'd visited were for adults only, though saying some females on them weren't underage might be walking a thin line." She was going to have to tell Thomas, after all. "One girl on one of his 'favorite' sites, he thought he recognized."

"Oh, God." Thomas's face contorted in horror. "From here?"

Dana empathized with that reaction. Her own had been about the same. "He wasn't sure about her, but if so, I'm afraid she is," Dana said. "One of Quinten and Katherine Windermere's exchange students."

"Which one?" Thomas asked. "They've had dozens over the years."

"Josie Rodriguez."

"Who?"

That he didn't remember her wasn't surprising. She'd been enrolled for such a short period of time. "She worked part-time for

Sylvia, and left without notice." Dana tugged at his memory. "Family emergency."

"Ah, yes. I recall." He frowned and lifted a hand. "You said Travis thought he recognized her. If he wasn't sure, maybe he was wrong."

"Maybe." Another loss? She couldn't take it. No, no, she couldn't afford to think that way. Vinn was in jeopardy. His whole future. For her, right now, all efforts had to be on straightening this out with Vinn and getting him out of jail and back in school.

"Dana, look now or you're going to miss it." Thomas motioned toward the sun.

Dana emptied her mind and looked out over the water at the sunset. "Gorgeous." It was amazing, shimmering soft pinks and peaches on the water.

When the sun slipped below the horizon, Thomas let out a low groan. "For years, it's been so peaceful here. Now, we seem to have a lot of family emergencies."

Family emergencies, crises, a murder. The worst part was, Dana feared, they were due for far more.

Chapter 15

Wednesday, October 10

DANA ARRIVED at the police station fifteen minutes early. Chilled to the bone in a lightweight black sweater and rust-colored silk blouse and slacks, she had stopped by The Grind and picked up coffee for herself and Laney certain that, barring an emergency, McCabe wouldn't be at the office this early in the morning.

Her nose numb, and no doubt red, she entered the station and saw Laney waiting for her, her long blonde hair pulled back in a ponytail. "I thought you could use a break from the usual sludge."

Laney looked delighted. "Thanks." She took the cup, then nodded toward the hallway leading to the interview room. "I woke Vinn early so he'd have time to clean up before you got here."

"Sorry you had to come in early."

"No problem." Laney leaned against the front desk. "I need to remind you that I can't speak to Vinn. His parents and attorney approved for you to speak to him as his psychologist, but I can't speak to him about the case or anything related without them being present."

Because he was a minor. "I understand."

"I'll take you back then." Laney set off across the open expanse and headed down the hallway.

Dana followed and entered through the door Laney held open. Its hinges creaked. "Vinn, Dr. Perkins is here to see you."

Dana smiled and then walked past Laney and entered. Vinn sat in one of four chairs at a small square table, his back to the wall. Dana set down her things, hearing the door close behind her. "Hi, Vinn."

"Dr. Perkins." He dipped his chin, his cheeks ruddy and his brown hair neatly combed. "Thank you for coming to see me."

"It took a while to get the approval, or I would have been here sooner."

His hazel eyes seemed clouded. He was glad to see her, but embarrassed at the circumstances. That, she totally understood. Vinn wasn't the image conscious type Thomas was, but he was well aware of the importance of reputation. "I'm not sure why you're here," he said.

Dana held her smile. She had to work at it. "I'm here because I thought you probably needed someone to talk to about all this."

"Mom and my dad come see me every day."

"Are you able to talk freely to them?"

He shrugged.

"I know you're innocent, Vinn," Dana said softly. "I know it, so you don't need to pretend with me that you killed Sylvia. We can just talk. I'm not here as your principal. I'm here as your psychologist."

That sparked his interest. "Medical privilege?"

She nodded.

"Okay." He thought it over. "Okay, then. We can talk." Hunched over the table, he straightened. "This is good."

She hoped so. "So let's start with you telling me why you confessed to this crime you didn't commit."

"I did do it." He lifted a defiant chin so like Thomas's.

Her smile faded and she let him see how serious she was in a level look. "We're not going to get very far if you lie to me."

"I'm…not."

Dana scooted closer to the table, took a sip from her coffee, and set the cup back on the tabletop. "I know you're lying, Vinn, and I don't appreciate it."

"I'm sorry you're upset, Dr. Perkins. I guess I let you down, too."

She squeezed her hands, lacing her fingers. "I'm going to say this once, and only once, so you hear and listen to me." She waited until he looked her in the eye. "I said, I know you're innocent. Why you're claiming you killed Sylvia, I don't know. But you didn't do it."

He grunted. "How do you know that?"

"Because I know you."

"I did it, okay?" Agitated, he set out to prove his guilt to her. "I went over there and…and I did it."

"You didn't." Dana calmly sipped from her cup, wishing they could skip this part of confrontation and denial, but it was a necessary step to getting beyond it.

For the next thirty minutes, they argued back and forth, him professing his guilt and her declaring his innocence. And she was certain of it. Could she prove it? Not really. Not yet. But no doubt lingered in her. His defense was so staunch, his conviction and determination to be blamed so severe…and not one single detail. An entire description of the murder, and not one single detail.

Vinn hadn't been there at the time of the murder. He couldn't tell her what he didn't know, which meant he had to be covering for someone very important to him. One of his parents? Kristina? Someone else he felt a deep desire to protect?

Finally, Dana saw the signs he was ready to progress and shifted tactics. "It doesn't matter how many times you say you did this, or what words you use, or how loud your voice gets, Vinn. None of that changes the facts."

"You hear me but you are not listening." He lifted a hand and let it fall onto the table. "Don't you always say we need to hear and listen? Didn't you tell me that a little while ago? Well, so do you."

"I hear your every word, and I will listen, when you start telling me the truth."

He glared across the table at her.

Checking her watch, she went on. "I know where you were that night, Vinn."

"What?"

"I know you met Kristina."

"Oh, man." The color leaked from his face. "That was after," he insisted, thinking fast.

"Vinn," Dana dropped her tone to just above whisper, where he had to really focus and strain to hear her. "You couldn't have been at Sylvia's at the time of the murder. You were at the other end of the street, meeting with Kristina. Everyone thought you two were just friends, but you're not. It's more than that."

He shut his eyes, slumped in his seat.

"What I want to know is why you're ruining your life, saying you killed Sylvia when you didn't."

His eyelids snapped back and anger flooded his face. "She needed killing."

The ferocity in his tone surprised Dana. It shouldn't have. To confess to murder required strong and intense emotions for non-psychopaths. And Vinn certainly wasn't a psychopath. "Did she hurt you or someone you love?"

His jaw tightened and his lips went flat, pressed together hard.

"I know you were angry with Sylvia, and I know you two had harsh words. Why did your feelings for Sylvia change? You had such respect for her when you did your project."

"That was about her business, not about her," he insisted. "Respect her? I hate her—and she is the reason things changed. Not me."

"No doubt." Dana observed him carefully. His body language, his tone, his mood. "Mr. Travis told me just today that you were his star student."

"Was." Bitterness seeped from him, spilling into the air between them. "Not anymore."

Reality had set in. He was in a bad situation here, and that remark proved any illusions he had of getting out of this unscathed had crashed. "I guess you heard Mr. Travis is no longer with us."

"I figured it out," Vinn said. "I heard Deputy Chief Holt on the phone. It's quiet in here. Her voice carries."

"I see."

"So is it true?" he asked her.

Good. Engaging outside of himself. "Is what true?"

"Is he saying he killed Sylvia?"

And that was a telling question. Dana tilted her head. "Vinn, if you had killed Sylvia, you wouldn't have to ask me that question."

He stood up, clenched his hands into fists at his sides. "I did kill her. I'm tired of telling you that."

"Fine." Dana stood up. "Show me how you killed her."

"I am not choking you, Dr. Perkins. I won't do that."

"Why not?"

"I won't do it!" He shouted.

Laney stood on the other side of the window at Dana's back. Making sure things didn't get out of hand. Uneasy at seeing them both standing, she knocked and quickly opened the door. "Everything okay in here?"

"We're fine, Laney." An idea occurred to her, and Dana ran with it. "Would you come in here, please?"

From the door, Laney addressed only Dana. "Dr. Perkins, I explicitly explained that I can't speak to your patient about his situation or case without parental permission or authorization from his attorney."

"I know." Dana reached for her handbag and fished out her phone, then started recording a video and positioned the camera where it showed all three of them. "Vinn," Dana said. "May I video this—to prove that Deputy Chief Holt has in no way violated her orders."

"Yeah."

Dana gave the time and date, and named those present in the room, stated the purpose of the video was to prove there was no unauthorized interaction during the meeting. "Deputy Chief Holt, will you come and stand right here, please?" She motioned Laney in the direct path of the camera.

Laney wordlessly stood in position.

"Both Vinn and I are aware you can't speak to him without consent because he's a minor. You don't need to speak at all. I just need a mannequin, if you will, and you're available. Is that okay with you?"

Skeptical, Laney nodded. Dana smiled, then asked Vinn. "Did you see Deputy Chief Holt nod?"

"I did." Vinn sounded as skeptical as Laney looked.

"Good. Now," Dana said, "I've asked Vinn to demonstrate the way he choked Sylvia. He wouldn't choke me—"

"You're the principal, Dr. Perkins," Vinn cut in. "I can't do that."

"I know, Vinn, and it's fine." Dana smiled to reassure him. "Deputy Chief Holt, would you stand still please and pretend you are Sylvia?"

Surprise and maybe a little respect flashed through Laney's eyes, and again she nodded.

"Okay." Dana double-checked the camera. "Perfect. Okay, Vinn. Show me."

His face flushed. "I can't do that."

"Why not?" Dana asked.

"I don't want to." Vinn shook his head.

"There are times in life when we all must do things we don't want to do, Vinn. This is one of them." She used her best school teacher's voice. Kids tended to respond to it innately. "Show me."

Resigned, he let out a sigh that slumped his shoulders. He stepped around the edge of the table, came up behind Laney, and then lifted his hands. He circled her, but didn't make contact between his curled fingers and her throat. "Like this."

Laney's eyes stretched wide.

"All right." Dana's gaze clashed with Laney's. "Thank you. You can sit back down now, Vinn." She tipped her head toward Laney. "Thank you, Deputy Chief Holt. You can go now. That's all I needed to see."

Laney left and closed the door behind her.

Dana reached over and turned off the recorder, placed the phone back in her handbag.

Vinn stared at her. "So now what?"

"Now, I have to get to school." She checked her watch—7:45. "But I'll be back this afternoon." Gathering her tote and cup, she looked up at Vinn. "Between now and then I want you to think."

Puzzled, his forehead wrinkled. "About what?"

Dana faced her student squarely, put a bite in her tone. "About whether or not you're going to continue to confess to a crime you didn't commit to protect someone else who is guilty and willing to ruin your life to keep their secret."

Vinn's jaw dropped loose.

He hadn't expected that. "I want you to think about this, too." She paused and took the heat out of her voice. "What kind of person would let you be blamed for a murder you didn't commit? Is that someone you *should* protect?"

He opened his mouth to say something, but no words came out.

Dana held up a hand. "Just think about what I said, okay?" She stared, waiting for his nod. When she got it, she walked out and closed the door behind her.

At the mouth of the hallway, Laney motioned to Officer Seth Trask. "He's ready to go back to his cell, Seth." When he passed and entered the interview room door, Laney spoke to Dana. "My office." She led the way.

When they were in her small office, Laney closed the door and sat down.

Dana remained standing. She really needed to get to school. "He didn't do it."

"I know. But how did you know?" Laney grimaced. "McCabe and I have repeatedly asked Vinn to show us how he strangled Sylvia. He wouldn't do it."

"He was afraid he wouldn't do it right and you'd know the truth."

"So why did he do it for you?" Laney asked.

"He told you. I'm his principal. An authority figure he has been trained for years to obey. Kids don't get to tell the principal no. So he did what kids do." Dana stepped closer. "You agree now that he's innocent."

"It's not enough, but it helps a lot," Laney admitted. "I shouldn't say anymore."

"You don't have to," Dana told her. "Sylvia wasn't strangled from behind."

"How do you know that?"

"I saw it in your eyes—when he stood behind you and reached for your throat. You were shocked."

"Can't dispute you there."

"Sylvia was strangled face-to-face," Dana deduced. "Someone she knew well and she trusted. Had to be for her to let them get that close." Pausing, Dana gauged Laney's reaction. She couldn't confirm or deny, but they both knew no sign was a huge sign. Dana was right, and some secrets meant to be kept had to be told. A killer was still on the loose in Shutter Lake, and she or he could kill again. "Wade Travis and the mayor...Sylvia was blackmailing them," Dana said. "Maybe others, too."

"Interesting."

She knew. It was in her eyes, and as much of a confirmation as Dana was going to get. "Neither of them did it, in my opinion."

"About Venezuela," Laney said. "I talked with Sylvia's parents. Both Zion and Yolanda separately."

"So have I," Dana admitted. "Sylvia had mentioned taking an extended vacation to Venezuela to them. Her father opposed it. Her mother thought it was long past time Sylvia took a vacation. She said she'd not been on one since opening Sparkle."

Laney didn't dispute her, so her information must have tracked with Dana's. "Why did her dad oppose, do you think?" Laney asked.

"He didn't say, but I looked online and the State Department has the whole country under a travel advisory alert. Things are a real mess over there. I expect maybe he was concerned for her safety." Dana let her gaze drift. "I'm almost sure she planned to go looking for Josie Rodriguez. She was on the list I sent of things to tell you."

"I got it."

"Did you look into her family there?" Dana asked.

"They're not in Venezuela anymore."

Shock pumped through Dana's body. "What do you mean? They moved, I know. But they left the country?" Quinten and Katherine Windermere had put the girl on a plane to go home for the family emergency. Katherine had told Dana so at the time.

"The Rodriguez family immigrated here. They live in Grass Valley now." A haunted look landed and stayed in Laney's eyes. "They wanted to be close to their daughter."

One town over. "Which explains why Josie was working part-time for Sylvia at Sparkle. None of the other exchange students had worked while with the Windermeres." No flight required. "How long have they been here?"

"They arrived about two weeks after Josie got to the Windermeres."

"So why was she staying with them?" With her family living so close by, that didn't make sense.

"She wasn't," Laney said. "Once her family arrived, Josie moved home."

Dana frowned. "But she was presented to us as an exchange student."

"She was an exchange student," Laney said. "But then the family got approved and they moved to Grass Valley, so she went home to live with them."

Dana processed these developments. "Mrs. Windermere. She wanted Josie in our Blue Ribbon school rather than in Grass Valley's system," Dana guessed. "So she just didn't tell us about the change in Josie's status or that she was living in another school district." They turned down out-of-district requests all the time. "That would explain Mrs. Windermere's recent unsolicited and sizable donation to the school library." Guilt money for the non-disclosure, to cover the added expense. Josie would have been transferred to Grass Valley.

"That was my guess," Laney agreed. "I ran a check. Something came up, so I called Grass Valley PD. It's a matter of public record, Dana."

"What is?"

Dread filled Laney's face. "Josie Rodriguez is listed as a missing person."

"Missing?" Dana felt her knees going weak. She sat down in the chair near Laney's desk. "Oh, no. For how long?"

Her expression warned Dana wasn't going to like the answer. "Since two days after the Windermeres supposedly put her on a plane for Venezuela due to a family emergency."

"Mrs. Windermere specifically told me that she and her husband had put Josie on that plane," Dana told Laney.

"Why would they do that if they knew her family was in Grass Valley?"

"They wouldn't." Dana had hoped not to have to disclose this, but there was no choice. "Wade Travis thinks he saw Josie, Laney. On a porn site. He isn't sure it was her, but if it was, he thinks she's been trafficked."

Laney buried her revulsion, but it sneaked into her body language. "What site?"

"Viva Venezuela, he said." Dana's mouth went dry. "Her stage name is Viva Vivian."

Laney jotted that down on a yellow pad, then paused to digest. "I'll look into that."

Only a fool wouldn't put it together. "Sylvia saw the site, too. Wade showed her. She wasn't sure it was Josie either but, I think that vacation she was planning was to go and find out. Sylvia was very protective of her employees." No travel advisory alert or food shortage would slow her down.

"I'll see what I can find out."

Dana's stomach burned. She pressed a hand to it. "Travis said he told Sylvia, if the girl was Josie, she could be anywhere. The site could be anywhere."

"They tend to move around."

The sites or the people? Dana didn't ask. She had enough night-mares. It wasn't that she didn't care about Josie. She didn't even know enough to be dangerous at looking for her. For Josie's sake, Dana put her in Laney's capable hands. Her priority was Vinn. It must remain Vinn. Getting him out of jail and back in school.

"When I talked with Sylvia's parents, I have to tell you, Laney, they couldn't get rid of me fast enough." It had struck Dana as odd then, and it did now. "Neither of them wanted to discuss her."

"Grief hits people in different ways."

"It does," Dana agreed. "But it doesn't usually scare them."

"What do either of them know about Josie?"

"I'm not sure," Dana admitted. "They knew her. They're in and out of Sparkle all the time. They talk to the girls who work for Sylvia, even bring them lunch sometimes."

"I'm going to speak to Renata Fernandez again and see what insight she can give me." As if remembering herself, Laney pressed her hands to her lips. "Just thinking aloud," she said. "I can't talk about the case with you, but I appreciate your sharing your impressions. You know these people in ways I don't."

Dana often found herself suffering from the same kind of restraints. "I brought you information I thought might be relevant. You haven't violated any protocols or ethics."

"Thank you." She nodded toward Dana's purse. "I need a copy of that video for our records, if that's okay? When Morris Barton hears I was in that room, he's going to go off like a Roman candle."

"That's why we made it. So he could see for himself you didn't do anything you weren't supposed to do." Dana pulled out her phone. "Give me the official email."

Laney reeled it off.

Dana attached the video and hit send. "There you go. Make sure you got it."

Laney checked, opened the file and ran through the video. "We're good."

"Great." Dana returned her phone to its slot in her bag.

"I appreciate your thinking to do that—making the video." Laney smiled.

"No problem. These days, covering everyone's back is a natural mindset. Comes with having to pay hefty malpractice insurance bills and an ever-present awareness, fear really, of legal liability."

"How well I know."

Dana hiked a shoulder, her mind racing. "You know, Connie

Bradshaw often talked with Julia Ford. They used to meet all the time at Fitzgerald's for lunch. Maybe Connie mentioned something to her."

"You think he's covering for his mother?"

"Odds are, but I don't know…yet." Dana checked her watch. "I've got to get to school. Pam will be overwhelmed."

"Travis matter?"

Dana nodded. "Email went out to the parents last night. I expect they're at fever pitch by now."

"Full throttle," Laney agreed. "Probably half of them are at your office."

"Exactly why Pam will be overwhelmed." Dana grimaced. "We're having all the parents in at three o'clock, but some will hit the office early to talk about their specific child."

"Maybe it won't be so bad. If it is, first round tonight at girls' night out is on me."

"Sounds like a plan," Dana said.

Laney stood up. "Thanks for everything."

Dana smiled. It was going to be a wickedly long day, but she could cope with it. Laney was now on the Vinn-is-Innocent train.

She left Laney's office with a spring in her step. What they had wasn't enough to clear Vinn, but they had made a huge step in the right direction.

Chapter 16

Perhaps Dana's certainty that she could cope with the wickedly long day had been a little optimistic. It had been wickedly long. But it also had been brutal.

She had expected accusations to be hurled and heaped on her head. She had expected concern and worry and even fear. She hadn't expected one of the mothers to stand up and shout, "Travis probably killed Sylvia Cole. Vinn's taking the blame because Travis is making him. I've read all about how these traffickers groom kids into doing what they want."

That set off a firestorm of screamed opinions and deepened fear in some and fury in others. Dana's stomach burned like fire and a dull ache pounded at her temples. She let them vent for a brief few minutes that seemed hours long. Thomas Jessup and all the others on the Shutter Lake Council had stayed seated at the table at the front of the gym and didn't seem inclined to intervene. That others were drawing the conclusion Vinn could be innocent was a good sign. But convicting Travis?

Dana lifted a hand, which was promptly ignored. Out of patience, she shouted. "Enough!"

The gym fell silent.

Never, not once in seven years, had she raised her voice to the students, much less at their parents. She stepped to the right, stood in the clear line of vision of the parent who had shouted the accusation out about Wade Travis. "With all due respect, kindly refrain from making false accusations against others. Any others," she said. "Mr. Travis has an alibi and is not a person of interest in the death of Sylvia Cole." She pointed toward Laney. "As Deputy Chief Holt will verify."

"That is correct." Laney said in a clear, loud voice.

"Now." Dana turned back to the parents and put the principal-authority in her tone. "If we could change this situation, we would. We can't. We might not like this sordid activity touching our town, our school and especially our children, but we address the problems we have." She strode a short path between the table where Thomas and the council were seated and the rows of chairs, seating the parents. "Go home and talk with your children. The first thing we must know is if Mr. Travis told us the truth—that no children were even aware of his addiction. Then report back to my office your findings, whatever they are, as soon as possible." She stopped. "It is our fervent hope that Mr. Travis was honest and the children are blissfully unaware of his problem. But either way, we need to hear from all of you what the children have to say."

A hand shot up. A mom. "Yes?" Dana asked.

"What if something did happen?"

"Let us know immediately. We'll contact Deputy Chief Holt right away. From there, we'll see what needs to be done and do it."

She fired back another question. "What if my child needs counseling?"

Thomas stood up. "Whatever the children need, they'll get," he promised. "I would like to thank Dr. Perkins for taking swift and decisive action on this matter. As soon as she learned of the problem, she acted. Mr. Travis was sequestered in her office under her direct supervision until he was retrieved by medical personnel."

"He wasn't around the kids at all?"

"No." Dana looked the father speaking right in the eye. "Absolutely not."

"Can't ask for more than that," he said, then returned to his seat.

"Anyone else?" Dana took the next question, then the one after, not rushing the parents, but giving them the time they needed to work through all their uncertainties and to come to terms with events.

Finally, the last of the questions was answered, and Dana ended with, "Okay, we know what we have to do. So let's do it and report back to my office before three o'clock tomorrow. We'll follow up with an email and release all the findings so that we all know exactly what, if anything, we're facing beyond getting a new history teacher."

Satisfied, the parents began to file out of gym.

Thomas joined her. "You did well, taking all their questions. Lessens the odds of us being sued."

"Anyone can sue over anything," Dana reminded him. "I'm hoping they won't, but they might."

Zion Cole spoke from behind her. "They'd lose. You acted within two minutes, Dr. Perkins. No reasonable individual can expect you to act before you're aware that a problem exists."

Vernon Bradshaw rubbed at the back of his neck. "They could sue over hiring him." He looked at Dana. "I take it you reviewed his file and nothing about any of this showed up when you hired him."

"I didn't hire him," Dana said. "Mr. Travis was already contracted to teach here when I came to Shutter Lake."

"On us then." Vernon said.

"But I did review his file," she said. "For what it's worth, there is nothing in it that would have kept me from hiring him."

"Who did the background check?" Vernon asked.

"Sterns and Brown." Dana lifted a hand. "They've done all of them, and we've never had a problem."

"Until now." Vernon frowned. "I'll have a chat with Sterns. Get them to double-check all the existing employees, just so we can say we did."

"Good idea." Thomas nodded his agreement. "Can't hurt and could help."

Spotting Pam waiting to speak with her, Dana told the council and Laney, "Thanks for being here for this. If you think of anything else we can do as preventative measures, let me know." She hoped there was nothing that involved the kids. Her greatest fear was that the parents, particularly of the little ones, would reveal more than the kids needed revealed in quizzing them. That's why she had spent so much time answering their questions and giving them examples of how to talk to the kids about this.

The council members left, including Thomas. Laney paused and touched Dana's sleeve. "You okay?"

"Oh, yes."

"Okay. See you back at the station," Laney said. "You're coming back to talk to Vinn again, right?"

"Absolutely." Holding onto that hope of getting him to open up and tell her the truth is all that had kept her together today.

Laney left and Pam stepped over to Dana. "I think I'd best stay around for a while."

"Why?"

Her eyes seemed huge and soulful. "The parents are going to go home, talk to the kids, and then they'll call to unload."

"Give them time to think things over first," Dana said. "You go home and dig in the dirt or listen to music or do whatever you like to do to relax."

"But—"

"No, Pam. Thank you," Dana said with a smile. "I appreciate what you're doing, but tomorrow is going to be an incredibly trying day. We both need to be fresh and ready for it."

She nodded. "Whatever you say, Dr. Perkins."

Dana left the gym, stopped by her office and collected her hand-bag. "I'm going now, Pam."

Seated at her desk, Pam nodded. "Tell Vinn I said hello. See you in the morning."

"I will." Dana was encouraged. So far, no calls. It'd been less than an hour, but most of the parents likely hadn't made it beyond the parking lot before phoning their upper-level students. It was the

VICKI HINZE

little ones that would be most difficult, but if any came in from that group, it'd be tomorrow.

Of course, keeping the parents calm was a fantasy. They would soon be in an uproar all over again. Once Dana convinced Vinn to tell the truth, and they realized he was innocent. They would be relieved about that.

Until it hit them that Vinn's innocence meant a killer was still on the loose.

Chapter 17

Catching a delicious whiff of cinnamon and spice, Dana noted the sign in Batter Up Bakery's window—Pumpkin Pie Cupcakes with Cream Cheese Frosting—and dropped in for half a dozen. Heidi typically only made those after Halloween through the new year. Pumpkins must be ripening early this year.

Heidi stood on the opposite side of the counter. In her black-and-white uniform and wearing her chef's hat, she took Dana's order and warned her, "Nothing low-cal about these, Dr. P., just so you know."

"Don't worry, they're not all for me." Dana smiled and paid for the purchase.

"Just didn't want the health nuts chewing on me." She sniffed and passed the pink-and-white box across the counter. "Trouble with the council, I do not need."

"No one does," Dana said in a conspiratorial whisper. It was the truth. Powerful men and women who were also brilliant and very specific on the community they wanted in Shutter Lake were impossible to thwart. You either agreed with them or suffered their wrath.

That was certainly no secret.

Fortunately, they also happened to be well-grounded, good

people. If not, few would thrive in Shutter Lake, and many had done very well here.

"Seeing the mayor, huh?" Heidi prodded.

"Actually, I'm going to see Vinn."

Heidi didn't look at all surprised. In fact, she seemed to be expecting it.

"Heidi?" Dana nudged her.

Her cheeks pinked. "Connie Bradshaw was in this morning. Actually, I baked the cupcakes for her. They're her favorite, and after I upset her, I thought she could use a little comfort food."

"That was very thoughtful of you." The discussion brought Troy Duval to mind. "Have you been to Mr. Duval's today?"

"First thing this morning." She smiled. "I was surprised. He seemed so happy to see me. Well, it wasn't me. It was the bagel. Said it reminded him of the many kindnesses Sylvia had shown him. We talked a solid half-hour." Heidi laughed. "He has a wonderful sense of humor."

"I'm so glad to hear that."

"I promised to come see him this weekend. He's rather frail," Heidi whispered, though there was no one else in the bakery this late in the afternoon. "I think you were right, Dr. P. The man is starved for company but he can't get out and around."

Heidi loved to talk and no doubt Troy Duval was tired of hearing his own voice. Sounded like a good combination for friendly visits to Dana. "Well, I think it's terrific for both of you. He's an astute businessman. Can't hurt to ask him to share his wisdom."

Her eyes gleamed. "I'll do that," she said. "I've been thinking about trying a little expansion."

"Do you need to expand for cupcakes?"

"No," she said. "But when I was a kid, my mother and I would go to New York twice a year. We always had high tea while we were there." Her expression went dreamy. "I loved high tea." She shrugged. "We don't have anywhere in Shutter Lake that serves high tea."

Dana sensed her excitement. It shimmered through Heidi and

felt palpable. "That sounds lovely. You should run the idea past Mr. Duval and see what he thinks."

"I will. I've dreamed of it for a long time, but you know how that goes. You do well and coast along and, before you know it, another year has gone by."

"I do know," Dana said. She'd done the same thing on her summer adventures, traveling. "Well, if you don't want to be having this same conversation next year, you best do something about it. Talk to Mr. Duval and see what he has to say."

"You know what? I'm going to do that this weekend. And I've got this sugar-free recipe I've been wanting to try. It would be perfect for Mr. Duval. He has to watch his sugar, you know."

Expertise in exchange for sugar-free cupcakes. Sounded like a deal to Dana. "Good for you." Dana smiled and left the bakery, certain Heidi was going to pick Troy Duval's brain for hours this weekend. He'd be delighted. And so, too, would Heidi.

Outside, Dana crossed the street through Downtown Square Park and wound through the cobblestone trails to a bench near the other side. Her stomach pitched in a series of twinges, so she grabbed an antacid tablet from the roll in her handbag and popped it into her mouth.

Two young mothers pushed strollers near the fountain. They'd been high school seniors her first year here. Close friends then, and now. Loving seeing that, Dana reached for her phone. Sylvia's parents intrigued her, and she'd spent the wee hours last night looking into their lives before Shutter Lake, but she hadn't stumbled onto that special something that her instincts warned her was there. She needed more current insight, and so she dialed Renata Fernandez's number.

Renata had been running Sparkle since Sylvia's death. Devoted to the job and to Sylvia and the standards she had set—or that everyone thought she'd set, being the Chamber of Commerce's Business of the Year two years running. If anyone could offer insight into any of the Coles, it'd be Renata.

"Sparkle Cleaning Service. Renata speaking. How may I help you?" Her thick accent sounded prevalent.

"Renata, this is Dana Perkins."

"Yes, Dr. Perkins?"

She was involved in some task. Her absence of focus was evident. "I wonder if I might have a moment of your time. It's about Sylvia."

"Of course," she said, fully focused now.

"I'm a little confused about something and I was wondering if you could help me get it straight in my mind."

"If I can, of course."

"Sylvia was so independent."

"She was, yes. Determined to make her own way without help from anyone else."

"Then why were her parents always at Sparkle?" Renata had disclosed that in their prior discussion. Dana hadn't really thought about the conflict until later.

"She was their only child. Mrs. Cole, she loves to cook. She considers all of us who work for Sylvia her girls. So she cooked lunch for us many days. Mr. Cole, he delivered it."

"Zion Cole delivered lunch to you girls?"

"Yes, a couple of times a week." Renata paused, then added, "To be honest, it was a little nerve-wracking."

That stunned Dana. "Why?"

"Don't get me wrong. Mr. Cole was always very nice to us. He's a kind soul…"

"But…?"

"But he asks many questions—especially to the new girls. All about their families and friends. It makes some of the girls a little nervous."

Dana processed that. "Did they fear for their jobs or something?"

"Well, sure. Sylvia's generosity with her employees is well known. It's hard to get a job here. She had very high standards. The girls worried if they said the wrong thing, it would get them into trouble."

"I'm a little surprised he'd ask so many questions. Do you think he was just being kind?"

"I thought it was just kindness, and his way of showing an interest in his daughter's work. He and Mrs. Cole adored Sylvia. They would have given her the moon and stars if she'd wanted them."

She wouldn't take anything from them. That much Dana knew from Vinn's report.

"We all love the Coles. They are very good to us," Renata said. "Well, except for Josie."

"Josie?" Dana feigned ignorance.

"You remember her. She was an exchange student who lived with the Windermeres and worked for Sylvia part-time. Beautiful girl."

Dana's heart beat hard and fast. "Why did she quit?"

"She didn't say. One day, she just didn't come to work. We heard later her family needed her back home."

"But Josie didn't like the Coles?"

"Oh, no, she did," Renata said. "Josie loved Mrs. Cole. Mr. Cole, Josie thought, was a little too friendly. He never did anything he shouldn't have done, but the way he looked at Josie bothered her. She wasn't used to attention, I think, and she mistook his interest. When we talked about it, she seemed relieved. She said things like that are different in America than in Venezuela."

"Why would she quit without telling Sylvia?" That didn't make sense to Dana.

"Dr. Perkins, what's she going to say? Your father is too nice? Too friendly?"

"I can see where that would be an issue."

"Like I said, we talked about it and I explained he was just interested because he wanted to please his daughter. Josie was fine with him after that."

"No one said anything about it to Sylvia?"

"Of course not. Sylvia protects us. She would have had words with her father. We couldn't be the cause of trouble between her and her father."

And for that same reason, he had to have been just being nice, didn't he? Flirting with a young girl wouldn't be worth upsetting his only daughter over, and Sylvia, being independent and protective, would have been upset with him.

Her mind settled, Dana checked her watch. Three-thirty. "Thanks for clearing that up for me, Renata. If you should think of anything else that might help…"

"I will phone you, Dr. Perkins. We loved Sylvia and we miss her very much. She was good to us. Now, the Coles are being very good to us, too."

"So Mrs. Cole still cooks lunch for you girls?"

"Oh, yes. She's here a lot more since Sylvia is gone. I think being with us makes her feel closer to her daughter."

Renata likely was right about that. "What about Mr. Cole?"

"He doesn't come in at all. Mrs. Cole cooks in the kitchen here now, so he doesn't need to deliver. She says he's grieving Sylvia too hard. He can't be at Sparkle knowing his daughter is no longer here. The pain is too raw."

A father feels he's supposed to protect his daughter, and Zion had failed to protect Sylvia. It would be extremely difficult to be reminded of that when the guilt—justified or not—is already tearing him apart.

Dana empathized in ways only someone who has lost those under her protection could understand. Poor soul was in for a rough couple of years. Maybe a rough lifetime.

"Thanks, Renata."

"Anytime," she paused. "Dr. Perkins, we girls have talked it over and we want you to know we do not think Vinn did this to Sylvia."

"Why not?"

"We know the boy well. Murder is not his nature."

"Is there more?"

"Sylvia was fond of Vinn. It had nothing to do with his parents. He was just a bright boy and she respected him for being determined to make something significant out of his life. With his parents, he wouldn't have to do anything ever. But he didn't want that. She respected Vinn very much. When he wouldn't forgive her, it broke Sylvia's heart."

"Forgive her for what?"

"I do not know," Renata said. "Sylvia would not talk about it, but she said she had hurt him and he wouldn't forgive her. She cried, Dr. Perkins. Sylvia never cried, but she cried at hurting Vinn."

"So because she cried you think he wouldn't hurt her? Even though she hurt him?"

"No. Because he respected her, too, and something happened, and he didn't respect her anymore. That's why I do not think he would do this."

A twisted crime of passion says he could have, though he didn't.

"Vinn is smart and he is sensible. He avoids people he doesn't respect. He doesn't kill them."

She had a point there. He would and had avoided Sylvia. Refused to talk. Just walked away. "Thank you, Renata, and thank the girls for sharing their thoughts."

Dana ended the call and gathered her things, then made her way to Main Street and crossed near the police station.

Sylvia was an enigma. She was well liked but a blackmailer. Assertive and aggressive but so protective she'd confront her own father to protect her workers, or travel to a foreign country to make sure a worker was okay when she wasn't positive the person was her worker. And she'd hurt Vinn and been so upset she had cried that he wouldn't forgive her.

Definitely a complicated woman.

Chapter 18

Before the door closed behind Dana in the police station, Laney intercepted her. "Vinn's parents are here. I've kept them out of sight."

"Okay." Why this was significant, Dana didn't yet know. "Haven't they both been in every day since his arrest?"

"Every day. His dad, sometimes twice a day. McCabe's given them free access to Vinn. Figures it's good for them and for the boy."

"I see." She happened to agree, though McCabe's opinion surprised her. She figured he would come down a little more hard-line. Glad she was wrong, she waited for Laney to explain.

"They already gave permission for you to talk to him, and now they're willing to let me listen in."

"You told them you believe he's innocent."

Laney nodded. "I still can't say anything—their vulture lawyer, Morris Barton, expressly forbade it—but I will have the sound inside the room turned on. I wanted you to know it. The Bradshaws and I will be listening."

"You realize I should refuse."

"No, you shouldn't. Because our goal isn't to violate medical privilege, it's to get Vinn out of jail."

"I have to tell him."

"Then tell him this conversation isn't private. He understands that. Just don't tell him his parents are listening. McCabe is with them. I'm going now, I just wanted to let you know first." Laney lifted a finger. "Oh, and Vinn doesn't know that Wade Travis has an alibi."

Dana passed her the cupcakes, and then opened the box. "I'm taking one to Vinn."

Laney hesitated only a second. "Fine."

Dana pulled one out of the box. "Heidi says they're Connie's favorites. Feel free to share. The rest are yours."

"Thanks." Laney smiled. "Get him to talk to you Dana. He is our best chance for helping him."

"So I'm clear. You want me to keep the alibi information from Vinn?"

"You're free to disclose that we're looking at Wade Travis on Sylvia's case."

"I see." She started to ask if that was true, but she really didn't want to know.

"Vinn's waiting for you in the interview room."

"Okay, then." Dana walked across the open expanse then down the hallway to the interview room. She opened the door. "Hi, Vinn."

"Dr. Perkins." He groaned. "I know you're not coming in here with a pumpkin cupcake you're going to eat in front of me."

She laughed. "How did you know it's pumpkin?"

"Mom loves them." He tapped his nose. "I know the smell."

Dana pulled a napkin from her tote and placed the cupcake on it on the table before him. "I hoped you'd like them, too."

"Love them." He smiled the first genuine smile she'd seen from him. It did her heart good.

He sank his teeth into the cupcake and mumbled an appreciative groan. "These are so good. Thanks for bringing me one."

"Say thanks to Deputy Chief Holt for letting me bring it in to you. She'll hear you. This meeting isn't private."

"Thanks, Deputy Chief Holt." He paused to chew slowly. "You okay, Dr. Perkins?"

"Well, to be perfectly honest, it's not been one of the better days of my life. But tomorrow is another day, so that's not important. You are what is important to me."

"You know, Dr. P., I've seen a lot of teachers love their students. But not like you. We talk about it all the time. You're all about us. In everything."

"You guys notice that?"

"Well, yeah." He seemed amused that she wasn't aware. "Everybody knows it."

"And that's okay with you guys, right?"

"Well, sure." He seemed bewildered. "A lot of the kids don't have anyone at home who believes in them, but it's okay, because everybody knows you believe enough for the rest of the world."

Her jaw dropped loose. She shut it.

He laughed out loud. "This is a kick. You have no idea how important you are, do you, Dr. P.?"

She guessed her clueless expression gave her away.

He guffawed. "Why do you think we study so hard? We stay out of trouble?"

Dana wasn't sure. She took a stab at it. "Because you'll get put on restriction?"

"No, they have to love us. They're our parents," he said then stilled. "You don't. We don't want to disappoint you."

"Me?"

"You believe in us, Dr. P." He was all kinds of serious now. "When Matt Tyler's dog died, you sent him a sympathy card and wrote one of your corny sayings in it."

"That was a Plato quote."

"Yeah," he said. "Who does that? Pooch was just a dog to everybody else. But you knew he was Matt's best friend. We all loved that dog."

"Matt told you about the card?"

"He still carries it around in his backpack." Vinn took another bite of cupcake. "We love those things you do."

"The corny sayings."

"The quotes," he said. "That you do stuff for us you don't have to do. It's cool."

Dana was about to fall out of her chair. Students respect their principal. And fear being reprimanded by her. They don't usually react like this, and she wasn't sure it was a good thing. "So I should quit the quotes, then?"

"No way." He looked horrified. "We like them."

"Which one is your favorite?" Dana used quotes all the time. They conveyed a lot in a few easy-to-remember words.

"The one about truth," he said after thoughtful consideration, then polished off the rest of the cupcake.

And that was her opening. She folded her hands together atop the table. "I'm glad you value the truth so much. It bodes well for your future."

For a moment, he had forgotten where he was and his circumstances, but that remark hit him like a ton of bricks. "I guess I've really disappointed you."

Dana avoided responding to the question. "Did you do what I asked and think today?"

He nodded. "All day. Really."

"Good." Dana pushed. "So are you ready to tell me who you're protecting?"

"Nobody." The light in his eyes dimmed.

There wasn't as much defiance or resolve in his voice as there had been this morning. Remnants remained, but he was weakening. "Can I be honest with you, Vinn?"

"You're always honest, aren't you?"

"I try to be," she said. "I guess a better word choice would have been blunt. Can I be blunt with you?"

"Sure."

"It's been a hard day, after a hard day. Actually, it's been hard days since Sylvia was murdered, and I'm really worn out. And, putting it bluntly, I've had about enough of people and their secrets."

"I don't like secrets either," he said, hurt shining in his eyes. "Mainly because they never stay secrets."

"I've treated you fairly, haven't I?" she asked. Before he could respond, she shot another question to him. "Have I ever lied to you?"

"Not that I know of."

"I haven't," she said flatly. "Why do you think that is? Never mind. I'll tell you why. I respect you, Vinn. I respect all of my students."

"I know. You tell us that all the time."

She frowned a rare frown. "So why are you disrespecting me?"

"I'm not—"

"You are," she insisted. "I know Deputy Chief Holt is looking at Mr. Travis to see if he's Sylvia's killer. You even asked me if he did it. I know you didn't do it. So why don't you stop disrespecting me and tell me the truth?" Realizing her voice was elevating, she paused and calmed it. "This is your life, Vinn. Your whole life is being decided by you right now. And so far you're not making wise decisions." She raised her hands. "I don't get it. You're smart. Far too smart to settle for illogical decisions."

His eyes burned. "You don't get it."

"Then explain it to me so I do." She challenged him. "I want to get it. I'm wracking my brain trying to get it. Help me."

"I can't!" he shouted.

Dana leaned even further toward him. "Yes, Vinn. You can. Do it!"

"It's my mom. Okay? My mom!" He covered his mouth with his hands. "Oh, man. I can't believe I...forget that. Dr. Perkins, forget that."

"You can't believe you told me the truth?" Dana sat back and let the silence between them fill the room. "You're a good son, Vinn. You're protecting your mother. I get that. But I know you were seriously angry with your father. "

"Who told you that?"

"No one told me. I saw it. In everything you said, and in what you didn't say."

"You'd be mad at him, too. He ruined everything." Vinn shut his mouth, tightened his jaw. "This is all his fault."

"What exactly is his fault?"

Silence.

"Vinn?"

Still silent.

"Vinn, I know," Dana whispered. "You might as well tell me so we can talk about it."

Tears welled in his eyes and he spat out the words. "It's his fault my mom killed Sylvia."

In her mind, Dana saw Connie Bradshaw scrambling to get out of whatever room she was in and into this one, and McCabe and Laney holding her back. Swallowing hard, Dana reached into her tote and grabbed a tissue, passed it to Vinn. "Why do you think your mom killed Sylvia?"

"You said you know. Why do I have to tell you?"

"Because it's important to me to hear what you think."

He swiped at his face, wadded the tissue into a tight ball. "I was there working on my report with Sylvia. My mom didn't know I was there. She showed up, and Sylvia told me to hide in her bedroom. So I did."

"Were you intimate with Sylvia?"

"God, no. She's beautiful, but old." His face flushed. "I shouldn't have said that. I mean, she's too old for me."

"You're right," Dana said.

"I was just staying out of sight. My mom would have been ticked off at me for being there."

"Why? If Sylvia was just helping you with your report...?"

"Because my dad was messing around with Sylvia," Vinn said. He shook his head, his expression contorted in anger. "Can you believe that? I thought she was my friend. I thought he loved my mom. She's so good to him and he goes and messes around with Sylvia. What's wrong with him?"

"So Sylvia and your mother argued."

"Oh, yeah." His exaggerated movements proved it'd been a wicked one, too. "Sylvia tried to calm Mom down. She told Mom not to worry about it. Their affair was over." His voice choked. He paused and cleared his throat. "My mom was so hurt and angry. She was crying all the time. And my dad just kept acting like nothing was wrong. I heard him tell my mom it didn't mean anything." Vinn looked disgusted. "I wanted to put my fist through his face. It meant plenty to my mom. Enough that she went back over there and killed Sylvia."

"How do you know that, Vinn?"

"You didn't see Mom, Dr. P. I did. She was worse than mad and hurt. She was sick with it." He let out a shuddered breath. "She killed Sylvia."

The door opened behind Dana. She looked and saw Connie Bradshaw enter the room. "I didn't kill Sylvia, Vinn." Tears streamed down her face. "I was hurt and angry and sick with it but, I promise you, I didn't kill her."

"Mom, just tell the truth," he told her. "I heard you say you were going to."

"I did say it, but I didn't kill her."

Vernon Bradshaw stepped around Connie and faced his son. "Neither did I. I swear it." His eyes brimmed with tears. "Vinn, I am so sorry for the pain I've caused your mother and you. What I did was wrong. I said it was nothing, but you were right. It was a huge thing. My family trusted me, and I broke that trust." He gripped the back of an empty chair, his knuckles turning white from a tight squeeze. "What I did was unforgivable. I am so sorry."

Connie stepped closer to Vernon, placed a hand on his shoulder. "We're both sorry, Vinn."

"Neither of you killed her?" Inside, Vinn was reeling. It showed. He crossed his chest with his arms and plucked at his sleeves, as if his nerves were on the outside of his skin and agitated. "Neither of you?"

"No." Connie promised.

"No, Vinn," his dad said.

"I didn't kill her either." Finally, Vinn said aloud the words Dana had been waiting to hear.

The tears blurring Dana's vision slid down her face, and she took her first easy breath since this nightmare had begun.

Given a signal by McCabe, Connie and Vernon embraced Vinn.

Dana and Laney backed out of the room and walked a short distance down the hallway. Out of earshot of McCabe and the Bradshaw family, they stopped.

"Maybe Connie did do it," Dana said, voicing her greatest fear.

"She didn't," Laney said. "She was in Grass Valley all day having liposuction, trying to stay young looking for a man who didn't appreciate her."

After that kind of surgery, no way was she out strangling Sylvia the same night. "What about Vernon?"

Laney lifted a shoulder. "His current assistant says he was in the office until 10:00 PM, then he met a couple of buddies for drinks at The Rabbit Hole."

"Which buddies?"

"Mayor Jessup and Quentin Windermere. Ray Jones was tending bar that night. He says they were all there."

Dana and most of the women stayed away from The Rabbit Hole. It's black walls and ceiling and dark décor were too off-putting to them. "So he's in the clear, too?"

"Looks like."

Dana thought a long second. "Well, that clears Wade Travis, Mayor Jessup, Connie, Vernon and Vinn." Thomas was still half in love with Connie Bradshaw, which was probably why he had never married. He hadn't denied that. Oh, he'd had relationships, but as soon as a woman got serious, he was gone. Knowing that about him was one of the main reasons Dana had made it clear that they would be friends and colleagues, but never anything more. Honestly, the clotheshorse thing got to her. He had enough good points to stay on her friend list, but a romantic interest? That was so not happening. "It wasn't Kristina either," Dana told Laney. "She was with Vinn."

"Got that from your note, and she's verified it."

"So what happens now? Can Vinn leave?"

"No, we need more." Laney seemed sorry to admit it. "We found Vinn's DNA at the scene."

"He said he was there."

"In her bedroom." Laney sent Dana a flat look.

"What kind of DNA?"

"Seminal."

Dana shut her eyes. "He was in her bedroom. Was it—"

"Under her bed."

"Of course. Hiding out while his mother and Sylvia were arguing." Dana winced. "He'd rather die of embarrassment than admit he…"

"Yeah." Laney nodded. "That's the problem."

"Have McCabe ask him about it," Dana suggested. "Guys relate differently than Vinn would about this with you or me."

"Jacking off in her bedroom would be like a badge of honor between them? Is that what you're saying?"

Dana avoided a direct response. "McCabe will know how to handle it."

Laney went back to the interview room, McCabe stepped out and she spoke briefly with him. A few minutes later, Connie and Vernon came out and McCabe grabbed two Cokes then closed the door.

He and Vinn. That was it. Maybe, just maybe, Vinn would talk straight to McCabe and end this.

A long half hour later McCabe came out and sent Vernon and Connie back into the room. He came down the hallway and joined Dana and Laney.

"Well?" Laney prodded.

He smiled. "I'm satisfied. We have no issue with the DNA."

"Sylvia didn't—"

"No, Laney." McCabe went serious. "We still have to wait for the forensics. Can't release him until the report is in, but Morris Barton needs to get down here and pull the confession."

"I'll call him," Laney said.

One step closer. Dana hooked her handbag on her shoulder. "Now what?"

Laney smiled. "Girls' night out—right after I call the lawyer. Then tomorrow, another press conference—five o'clock."

Dana nodded. Time to rattle a few more bushes. Hopefully they'd shake loose the killer…before he or she struck again.

Chapter 19

Dana looked beyond the long wooden tables with their fanned napkins and red glass candles to the door and watched Ana rush in. She spotted the three of them—Laney, Julia and Dana—seated at the back table near the windows and joined them, still wearing her white lab coat. "Sorry I'm late."

Ana was always late. It went with the territory of being a doctor.

"As I live and breathe," Julia said, smiling at her. "You're here before we pop the cork on the second bottle of wine tonight. I'm impressed, Ana."

She laughed good-naturedly. "Dana, I hear Vinn un-confessed."

"Withdrew his confession," Laney corrected her, and filled her glass with white wine.

"So Vinn withdrew his confession?" Ana corrected herself and dropped onto her seat.

"He did." Dana was still positively ecstatic about that.

"I know you're relieved." Ana asked. "So he's home with his family, then?"

"Not yet." When Ana looked to Laney for an explanation, Dana reminded the good doctor, "Laney can't discuss the case."

"Ah, of course."

"They can't let him go until they get a clear coroner's report."

"When is that due in?"

Dana again responded, sparing Laney. "Sometime tomorrow. Hopefully, before the press conference."

Julia paused, her glass mid-air. "There's another press conference tomorrow? Why do I not know these things?"

"Five o'clock," Dana said. "Will you be there?"

"After the last one, I wouldn't miss it." Julia shrugged off a reprimanding look from Laney. "What?" Julia asked. "Someone has to guard the doors for you and McCabe."

"Well, I know this," Dana said. "I'll sleep better once I know Vinn is home and back in school and this whole mess is behind us."

"That could be a while," Julia said, draining her glass.

Laney refilled it. "Why is that?"

"Where's Sylvia's killer?"

Laney frowned at her. "I can't discuss the case."

"She'll find him or her," Dana said. "One thing at a time. For me, my nightmare ends when Vinn is released."

"Unless it happens again."

"We're watching everything to prevent that." A steel edge honed Laney's voice to a razor's edge.

Julia dabbed at the corner of her mouth with a napkin and reached for a cracker then loaded it with Gouda cheese. "Well, I was at *The Firefly* office this afternoon, delivering some edits to my article, and I overheard a little tidbit that might interest you."

"What's that?" Laney asked. She wasn't in uniform. She wore dark slacks and a white silk blouse.

"You can't talk about the case," Julia reminded her. "So, Dana, I'm talking to you."

"Okay." Dana smiled and waited.

"Katherine Windermere came in asking to see Carrie Stone." They all knew Carrie was the owner of the weekly newspaper. "Katherine forgot Carrie was traveling in Europe, so I asked if I could help her. She said it was a confidential matter."

"That could be about anything," Dana said.

"Could be, but it wasn't." Julia sipped from her glass. "She wanted contact information for a computer hacker."

"A what?" Ana didn't bother to hide her surprise.

"Hacker. You know, someone who breaks into your computer, takes control of it, and charges you a bloody fortune to get it back."

"Not all hackers steal your access," Laney said.

"Or extort money from you to get it back," Dana said.

Julia conceded. "True and true. But in the world I worked in during my investigative journalism days, I learned a few things, too. Hackers rarely hack for the pleasure of it, though many do enjoy it. They usually have a purpose."

"I'll stipulate to that." Laney said.

Ana shot Dana a questioning look. "She agrees." Dana asked Julia, "So why did Katherine Windermere want a hacker?"

Julia's eyes twinkled, the same enigmatic shade as her natural blue turquoise earrings. "Now isn't that an interesting question?"

"Do you have an interesting answer?" Laney dipped her chin.

"Not yet. But I have a friend I'll ask to look into it. He's FBI. If he agrees, I'll let you know."

"I'd appreciate that." Laney refilled glasses, and noted Dana had barely touched her wine. "You planning on nursing that all night?"

"I'll take some more," Ana said, tilting her head toward Dana. "She's nursing her stomach, and she shouldn't be drinking at all."

Only a blind woman could miss the reprimand. Dana frowned. "Medical privilege." Dana called it, and issued a reprimand of her own. "You're not supposed to discuss my medical condition, Ana."

"Then you tell them. Ordinarily I'd agree, but this is personal and these are our friends. If we can't talk to friends about personal challenges…"

Julia cut in, ending the debate. "What's wrong with your stomach?"

"I'm fine." Dana groaned. "Can we not talk about it?"

Three pairs of eyes trained on her proved they would talk about it. Giving in, Dana shrugged. "A little too much acid. It's nothing."

"She's worrying about Vinn," Laney guessed. When Dana shot her a shushing look, Laney shrugged. "What? You are worried about him. You always worry about the students. It's a no-brainer deduction, not a Shutter Lake secret."

"Phoenix haunting your dreams again, Dana?" Julia asked, her concern genuine.

"I'm fine. Really," Dana said. "Like all of you, Sylvia's murder happening here was upsetting. That's all—and I have been worried about Vinn."

"Dana Perkins will fight to the death to protect the kids," Julia said. "Anyone on the lake can take that to the bank."

"She's good at it," Laney said, as if she weren't seated beside Dana, then glanced over at her. "I mean that. If I'm ever in trouble, I hope you're there on my side, fighting for me."

"That, you can take to the bank." Dana promised.

"I propose a pact." Ana held up her glass to toast. "Trouble comes for any of us, the rest are there."

"Pact." Dana added her voice to theirs and they all clinked their glasses.

Chapter 20

Thursday, October 11

THE NEXT MORNING, Dana sat at her computer completely frustrated. She'd come in at 5:15—The Grind opened at 5:00 and no way could she face today without a large Macchiato Espresso.

As soon as she arrived at school, she'd started searching hard for deep-background information on Quinten and Katherine Windermere. There had been a lot of articles posted and she'd waded through them, but she had found nothing that led her to believe they were anything but appropriate hosts for exchange students. She wrote up a report for her file, including all the article URLs, and then steeled herself and went to the website where Wade Travis had purportedly seen Josie Rodriguez or her lookalike.

The website was gone.

Dana's stomach burned as if torched with a hot match. On auto-pilot, she grabbed an antacid tablet from the roll in her top desk drawer, then tried the URL again.

Nothing. Not even an error message.

She slumped back in defeat. Travis had warned her that these sites disappeared frequently and without notice. So had Laney. Pam had captured screenshots of the home pages of the sites and certified them as true and correct copies for the file, but Dana had wanted to capture an actual Viva Vivian film clip to pass on to the police. Could the site owner have noticed an uptick in specific searches for Vivian? Was that the reason for the site's sudden disappearance?

The antacid kicked in and the burning in her stomach stopped. Dana slumped back in her chair and sipped at her coffee, then checked her watch—7:30.

Her desk phone rang.

"Dr. Perkins," she said on answering it.

"It's Laney," she said. "I've been calling you for hours. Do you ever spend time at home?"

Dana grunted. "I came in to look for a video clip on Josie— Vivian," she added in case the girl wasn't Josie. "The site is gone."

"Happens all the time. I'm not sure if we got one before it disappeared. Why did you want it?"

"For the file," Dana said. "In case any parents sue us over Travis."

"If we have a clip, we'll seek the necessary permissions and get you a copy. Provided they are granted. Can't see why they wouldn't be, if the school attorney requests a copy."

Dana scribbled herself a note to follow up on this, adding a new item to her to-do list. It was two pages long, and full of strikeouts and notes in the margins. Hieroglyphics on steroids that only she could decipher. "I dug around a bit on Quinten and Katherine, too."

"What for?" Cagy now, Laney gave away nothing in her voice.

"To make sure nothing in their pasts should prevent them from being exchange student hosts," Dana said simply. "Just to put my mind at ease."

"I didn't find anything on them either," Laney said. "If that helps."

"It does." Laney was a crackerjack investigator. If anything were there, she'd find it. "So why are you hunting me down at the break of dawn?" Pam entered the outer office and waved through the glass. Dana lifted a hand to return the greeting.

"The preliminary coroner's report is due in at about 2:30 this afternoon. I got a verbal on it, and it appears Vinn's in the clear."

Relief swept through Dana. "But the DNA?"

"McCabe isn't concerned about it. It's been adequately explained."

Dana understood. "No need for details," she told Laney, though she hadn't hinted specifics would be forthcoming. "So how did the coroner clear Vinn?"

"Morris Barton agreed to hand-casting samples. We did them and the coroner examined them."

"I don't understand." Dana frowned into the phone.

"The upshot is Vinn's hands are too small to leave the marks left on Sylvia's neck."

That Dana understood completely. "Wonderful news for Vinn." Dana enjoyed the burden releasing from her shoulders. She felt a hundred pounds lighter, without realizing the weight of all this had been that heavy. "I hope it's leading you to a specific someone else."

"Maybe." Laney sniffed. "Any calls from parents on Wade Travis?"

"Not even one, but it's early." Dana let her relief come through in her voice. "I'm praying hard the man told us the truth. We'll know by three o'clock." By then, word would be in from the parents on whether or not he had behaved inappropriately with any of the students.

"After talking with him, I think it'll be good news." Laney hesitated then added, "Vinn's going to have a hard time, coming back to school and facing his friends. Everyone will know about his dad cheating."

"No, he won't," Dana assured Laney. "I expected that. We had an assembly yesterday. I told the students there was a good chance Vinn would be released soon. The only thing he had done wrong was to not tell the truth. He confessed because he'd misunderstood something he'd seen and heard and he thought he was protecting someone else. Now he knows the truth, has told the truth, has been told what actually happened, so everything is fine."

"Did you tell them not to hound him about it?"

"More or less," Dana said, loving Laney's blunt way of hitting things head on. She so admired that about her. "I said it would be best for Vinn if others didn't mention the incident at all. This ordeal has been really hard on him, and as Vinn's friends and school family, we want to welcome him back and for him to be glad he is back. Not to make him uncomfortable."

"That should work. And, let me guess, you took questions."

"Dozens and dozens of questions, all of which I answered thoroughly without disclosing what happened or violating Vinn's privacy."

"Yeah, poor kid. Hard on any boy to see his family torn apart, but really hard on a mama's boy."

"Definitely, though he's more bonded with his dad than I originally thought."

"Really?"

"If he weren't, his dad's betrayal wouldn't have cut him so deeply. It wasn't just the impact on his mother that devastated Vinn, it was the impact on the family."

"Sounds pretty healthy."

"It is healthy. Kids should love both of their parents, and naturally, they gravitate at times to the one they perceive as the underdog in disputes."

"This was a pretty big dispute."

"Definitely." Dana accepted a cup of piping-hot coffee from Pam with a whispered thank you. When she exited the office and shut the door, Dana went on. "Can you imagine how torn up he's been?"

"No, but what I can imagine is it's the hardest thing he's ever faced in his life. It took a lot of guts for him to take blame. Don't get me wrong. It wasn't the right thing to do, but looking at it through his eyes, I get why he did it."

"When the heart and mind conflict, things get complex fast."

"Well, I'd say everything you can do, you've done. I hope the council appreciates what they've got in you, Dana."

"I don't know about appreciation, but they just renewed my contract, so I'm good for at least three more years."

"Congratulations."

"Thanks."

"Guess we'd better get back to it," Laney said. "See you at the press conference."

"When is McCabe going to let Vinn out of jail?"

"As soon as the report comes in, we'll start out-processing him. But Connie called this morning and asked us to hold off the actual release until the press conference is over. She's concerned people around town will say hurtful things to him if they haven't yet heard the truth."

"Good call." Dana wasn't surprised by Connie's request. She would have made it herself if she had thought of it. Of course, the kids had carried home everything shared in yesterday's assembly, so the point was probably moot anyway. What the kids knew, most of the parents knew, provided they listened.

"Nice work on all this, Dana."

The compliment surprised her as much as the one at girls' night out, especially after Laney's warning at Batter Up to stay out of her case and she would stay out of Dana's school business. Something had shifted. Mutual respect had deepened. "Thanks."

Dana hung up the phone then reached for her cup and resisted a palm-slap to her forehead. Friendship. That is what had changed.

Friendship and trust.

And mutual respect.

Chapter 21

By lunch, the parents had all reported in on Wade Travis. There were no reports of inappropriate conduct and all parents had been accounted for, so a relieved Dana notified Thomas Jessup.

The mayor was beyond delighted to hear the news, though Dana couldn't be completely certain if he was more delighted that the students had been spared or that the school wouldn't be facing lawsuits.

To his credit, he mentioned the students' safety first, which permitted Dana to be gracious and so she shared his relief on the latter. Thomas insisted he notify the council, which was fine by her. It only annoyed her a little that she wondered: If the report had gone the other way, would he have been as eager to be the council messenger?

The question did linger on her mind during lunch. Finally, she concluded that Thomas was Thomas and all about image and appearances. It had been drilled into him down to the nucleotides in his DNA, and she could either accept it and press on or resent it and press on. Considering it healthier, she chose acceptance.

Most of the afternoon, she watched the clock, eager for the press conference. Finally, five o'clock arrived and she gathered her handbag and tote, then left school and headed down the cobble-stone street toward City Hall.

Main Street was crowded. Half of Shutter Lake seemed to be gathering. Residents, and a lot of press. Even more press than had showed up at the first presser about Sylvia Cole's death.

Dana scanned the crowd and spotted Julia, waving her over. On the way to her and Ana, Dana saw cameras and call-letter logos from Grass Valley, Sacramento, and even one from Lake Tahoe in Nevada. That broadened interest by the media concerned her, but what she didn't see concerned her even more.

Not one student stood in the crowd to support Vinn.

"Where are all the munchkins?" Julia asked her.

Ana stood on the far side of Julia and leaned in to hear Dana's answer.

"I don't know," Dana said. "Everyone seemed all right after assembly, and they acted normal all day. I honestly thought they would be here for him." She couldn't hide her disappointment.

"Kids react to things in weird ways, Dana. You know that." Ana lifted a shoulder. "Not to change the subject, but I looked into that matter we discussed at my office."

"What matter?" Julia asked swiveling the clasp on her bracelet at her wrist.

"Josie Rodriguez," Dana whispered, then asked Ana, "Did you find anything?"

"Nada. Zip. It's like she never existed."

Dana's disappointment doubled. No kids here for Vinn. No news on Josie. Aside from the parental reports on Wade Travis, today had been a bust. But when Vinn walked through those doors, things were going to get a lot better. Glorious. "I bombed out, too," Dana told Ana.

"Let me guess. You discovered Viva Venezuela is no more," Julia said, her chunky stone necklace catching the sunlight.

"You've started looking at this, too?" Dana was surprised. Julia hadn't said a word.

"We made a pact and you asked me to, right?"

She nodded. But when she had asked, Julia hadn't wholeheartedly agreed. She'd left a high-profile job to get away from investigative journalism, though clearly she'd been good at it. The woman had a fistful of Gerald Loeb Awards and Pulitzer nominations. "Have you found anything?"

"Not a thing, which tells me something is very wrong." She lifted her spread fingers and wagged them. "My spidey-senses are on full-alert."

Ana frowned. "What are spidey-senses?"

"Spiderman senses," Dana translated, then shrugged. "The students use the term all the time."

"Ah." Ana nodded. "I'm surprised it hasn't come up at the clinic, but then I only see the little ones when they feel cruddy and we're focused on the physical."

"Ask them what their spidey-senses say is wrong. You might be pleasantly surprised at their answers." Dana asked Julia. "But you'll keep looking?"

"Isn't Laney looking into this now?" Julia dipped her sunglasses down on her nose and locked her gaze with Dana's.

"She is, but Laney's got to focus on Sylvia's murder." Dana lowered her voice so only they could hear. "We've got a killer loose, Julia. Of course that has to be her top priority."

"True." Julia waited.

She had an intense habit of doing that. Letting the silence stretch until you cracked and filled it. Even knowing what and why she was doing it, the tactic remained effective. "I know you don't like investigative work anymore, but Ana and I have done all we know to do. It wasn't enough. We're lost, Julia, and we need your help." Dana caught her up on all she had done, and Ana filled Julia in on her efforts, then Dana added, "At girls' night out, you mentioned an FBI friend who might look into…that other matter." Dana didn't want to say the Windermere's names aloud in this crowded group. "Maybe you could ask him for help. I think Vivian's situation is kind of their domain, isn't it?"

"Actually, it is. But they usually get requests from local authorities. Law enforcement can be kind of…territorial."

"Josie is officially a missing person and a minor," Dana said.

"That puts her case in the federal domain already. Maybe he could give the agent assigned to it a little nudge." Didn't hurt to ask. If Dana didn't ask, Julia wouldn't ask him, and it wouldn't get done.

Julia chewed on her inner cheek. "Just so we're clear. Neither of you is sure the girl you haven't seen in the video is even the same girl who is missing. But if she is the same girl, then you both think she's been trafficked."

"Sounds weak, but that's right," Ana said.

Dana nodded.

Julia continued. "You want me to locate the missing girl, get her back and to identify who trafficked her...even if it was someone in Shutter Lake. Is that right?"

Ana groaned. "It likely was someone from here. That's the only way the events we know have occurred make sense."

A killer and a human trafficker in America's perfect town? Chills swept through Dana. She stiffened. "We want the truth. Find the truth, Julia, please. Whatever it is and wherever they are. I hope it's not someone in Shutter Lake." Good grief! "But if it is, it is. We'll deal with it."

"All right then." Julia inched her glasses back up on the bridge of her nose. "For the record, I'm going to think twice about making any future pacts with you guys. When you need help, you really need help."

"Sorry, but thank you." Dana squeezed Julia's arm.

She sniffed again. "You know I left that life behind and came here to get away from it, right?"

"You mentioned it," Ana said.

"We all left lives behind and came here to get away from something," Dana reminded her. "But whether or not Vivian is Josie, she's a slave right now and, unless we help her, she's going to stay a slave until..."

"Stop." Julia lifted a hand. Her bracelet slid up her forearm. "I get the picture. Slave. Drugs. Dead. I've seen it too many times."

And she'd hoped never to see it again. "Look," Dana said. "I know Josie's ordeal is an entirely different case, and we have no proof of anything beyond her being missing and Travis maybe spotting her, but I believe all of this could somehow be connected to Sylvia's murder."

"Sylvia would never permit a woman or a girl to be trafficked, Dana."

"Julia's right," Ana said. "No woman, but especially not one who worked for her. No way. Sylvia bent over backward, trying to help them get better lives. She empowered women."

"I know all that," Dana told them. "But I've got this feeling." She rubbed a hand over her stomach. "I can't shake it."

"Spidey-senses." Julia's eyes gleamed interest. The war between what she should do and what she wanted to do raged in her and the battle played out across her face.

"Friends help friends," Ana reminded her.

Julia responded with a frown. "Okay, I said I'd help and I will. I'll do what I can—but only because no woman should be a slave, and because you two will owe me one. A big one."

Ana winked. "Dana's the Keeper of Secrets around here, and she actually does keep them." Ana snagged her sleeve on her lab-coat button, and worked to release it. "I've asked her at least a dozen times what happened that you left your job. She knows but won't say a word."

"How do you know she knows?" Julia narrowed a fierce gaze on Ana.

"It's in her eyes when I ask. But she won't say a thing." Ana looked peeved. "You should tell me yourself."

"I'm sure your imagination is far more intriguing than the truth," Julia said.

Dana smiled. "Thanks for helping Josie, Julia."

"I'll try. Doesn't mean I'll be successful," she warned Dana. "These cases don't usually settle out well. You understand what I'm saying, right?"

Slave. Drugs. Dead. "I do."

Skepticism crossed her face. "Is Travis's alibi airtight?"

"Supposedly." That was as far as Dana could go because it was all she knew. Laney hadn't revealed more.

"Understood. I'll dig deeper tonight then." Julia nodded. "But right now, I'm going to celebrate Vinn getting his life back. Too many kids mess up and never get a second chance."

Ana sniffed. "They don't have Dana fighting for them."

Dana appreciated the support, but with no kids showing up here today to support Vinn, she stood on shaky ground with herself. Why hadn't they come?

Glancing to the doors of City Hall, she spotted McCabe coming outside and then down the steps. He made his way to the podium and mic. Thomas positioned himself beside McCabe, wearing black and an understated tie. Formal and serious.

"Laney should be out here," Ana whispered. "It's her case."

Laney hated the attention and likely had coerced McCabe into doing it.

"If she wanted to be here, she would," Julia said. "You know Laney."

Dana agreed. McCabe cleared his throat, and she listened, giving him her full attention.

"Afternoon, everyone." McCabe introduced himself and the mayor for those unfamiliar, then set out the protocol of comments and then questions. "As you probably know by now, new evidence has come to light that proves the minor in custody who previously confessed to the murder of Sylvia Cole is innocent. We're processing his release as we speak."

"Why did Vinn Bradshaw confess?" a reporter shouted.

McCabe pointed at the man. "Shutter Lake is a small community, and while most know the minor's identity, hear me on this. You print any minor's name and we're going to have a problem."

"Why did he confess?" The contrite man repeated his question.

"Kids are kids." McCabe brushed past the question and said, "Next?"

An anchor from Grass Valley asked, "Did Wade Travis kill Sylvia Cole, Chief?"

McCabe took the question in stride. "Mr. Travis has an alibi."

Zion Cole pushed through to the front of the crowd, squared off at McCabe. "If it wasn't Vinn or Travis, then who killed my daughter?"

"We don't know yet, Mr. Cole," McCabe said. "But every avenue that can be explored is being explored. You have our word on that."

Zion's face contorted. "You need to light a fire under this investigation." He pivoted a glare between McCabe and Thomas. "Ramp it up."

"We've never ramped down," McCabe admitted. "We knew early on the minor in custody wasn't the killer. Dr. Perkins has been helping us sort through some confusion that was going on."

"Is Vinn all right?" A mother Dana recognized raised then lowered her hand, calling the question.

McCabe sighed at hearing Vinn's name. Dana had to withhold the same reaction. At least it wasn't Heidi Udall this time. She'd be really upset with herself for doing that again. Since Sylvia's murder, Heidi had been much nicer. Death could do that. Make a person self-reflect and re-examine their own lives. Dana hoped the changes in Heidi stuck.

"The minor is fine." McCabe assured the woman.

Zion charged the podium. "My daughter is dead. She's never going to be fine again. I want her killer found."

"We all do," McCabe said, exhibiting exaggerated patience. "And we are making progress on the case."

"Forget your progress. I demand results." His eyes widened. "I'm upping the reward." Zion elevated his voice and held up two fingers. "Two million dollars to anyone whose information leads to an arrest and conviction of the person who killed my daughter."

McCabe briefly squeezed his eyes shut. Dana didn't have to wonder why. Everyone in a five-hundred mile radius would be muddying up his investigation, trying to collect the reward. Julia's groan proved she realized that, too.

"Dana, look," Ana said, then nodded to the edge of the gathered group. "Look."

All of the children walked toward them, carrying signs that read: "Release Vinn."

Adults parted, making way for the students. They moved

between the adults, staying together, heading toward the steps of City Hall.

When they clustered at the foot of the steps, they began to chant. "Release Vinn! Release Vinn! Release Vinn!"

Dana glanced at McCabe. "We're done," he told Thomas Jessup.

Thomas smiled. "I'd say you better get the boy out here before they go in and get him."

McCabe went back inside. A few minutes later he and Laney held open the doors. Flanked by his parents, Vinn stepped outside.

The students began cheering. "We knew you didn't do it, Vinn."

Kristina stood in the front row. Her smile lit up the crowd and would have had it been pitch dark outside. "Dr. Perkins said from the start you were innocent."

"She was right." Vinn smiled.

Julia elbowed Dana. "Remember that. You don't hear kids say an adult is right often."

Dana chuckled, a little embarrassed at the attention.

Connie Bradshaw swiped at the tears streaming down her face. She'd been so afraid of Vinn being ostracized. Instead, he'd been embraced. She looked at Dana and mouthed, "Thank you." Then she looked at her son. Vinn flashed her a grin, and then sobered and focused on Kristina. "I didn't kill Sylvia."

"Why did you lie?" Heidi Udall asked him, her chef's hat bobbing with her head movements.

Dana winced and said sotto voice to Julia, "If she starts that blurting thing again, I'm going to lose my faith in human nature to ever permanently change."

"We all wear masks, Dana. You know that."

"We do." Dana cast an anxious look in Heidi's direction then crossed her arms over her chest and waited for Vinn's response. Truthfully, she too was curious.

"Because I didn't listen to Dr. Perkins." Vinn scanned the crowd and found Dana, then scrambled down the steps and hugged her hard. When he pulled back, he said, "She tells us all the time to just tell the truth. Not to be afraid of it ever." He shrugged. "I was afraid of the truth so I lied, and I made a mess. It took a while to straighten everything out."

He stepped back and looked at Dana. "I won't make that mistake again."

Too moved to speak, Dana held her smile. It trembled but she was okay with that.

"So you know," he told the kids, "Dr. P. believed in me even when I didn't believe in myself. She never gave up on me, and she wouldn't let me give up, either."

Julia clasped her arm and squeezed. "Well done, Dana."

A knot the size of a football lodged in Dana's throat. She blinked hard, swallowed twice. "All my students make believing in them easy." She cleared her throat. "The lesson in this is—"

"Just tell the truth," the kids shouted.

Guilt swept across the faces of many in the crowd, kids and adults. It took work—Shutter Lake was a land of many secrets—but Dana not only smiled, she laughed aloud.

Tell the truth. Such a simple lesson. She glanced from Vinn to Thomas. To Connie and Vernon Bradshaw, smiling with their arms locked at each other's waists, their heads bent together, their faces beaming at their son being treated well. Simple, yes. Yet, at times, so very complicated.

The Bradshaw family would be fine. Julia would look into Josie's disappearance, and Laney and McCabe would move heaven and earth to find Sylvia Cole's killer. Things were going to be okay. Vinn was safe, and tomorrow, he would be back in school, and life would go on in Shutter Lake.

Like the others, Dana had learned a valuable lesson: Knowing the truth is what is important. Sharing the truth may or may not best serve it. Wisdom comes in knowing what and when to share. Because some secrets you tell, but so many secrets should be kept.

Sneak Peek

ALL THE LIES

Enjoy this Sneak Peek of the next BREAKDOWN book *all the lies*, by Peggy Webb ©2018

Chapter One

Thursday, October 11

Only twenty days 'til Halloween. Julia knew. She'd counted. Every October for the last five years.

As if she needed any reminders, ghoulish carved pumpkins decorated doorsteps, faux bats hung from trees, and ghosts lurked in every dark corner of her neighborhood – the one she'd deliberately chosen when she moved here. Nothing bad could ever happen in a neighborhood on a street named Harmony. On a quiet street where kids tossed balls at twilight and mothers stood in doorways calling them to supper, where the blue-ribbon school was just a few blocks away and the police station was within easy walking distance.

For that matter, nearly everything Julia needed was within walking distance. Until now. Until Dana Perkins had pulled her out of a safe rut and asked her to dredge up investigative skills from a life she'd left behind. One of Dana's students at Shutter Lake School was missing, and she would not rest until the girl was found.

Less than an hour ago Dana had pressed her again about the girl as they stood in front of City Hall where Julia's instincts told her Chief of Police Griff McCabe was lying about closing in on a killer. Everybody in Shutter Lake was up in arms about the town's first murder. How could Julia refuse? Her adopted paradise was in an uproar and so was her friend. It wouldn't kill her to drag out her investigative reporting chops and try to find the girl, would it?

Julia shifted her bag to a more comfortable position on her shoulder as she strode toward her cottage, a modest craftsman where culinary herbs grew on the kitchen windowsill and light poured through the windows in every room. Lots of light. Julia couldn't stand the darkness. Nor the pumpkins. Those grotesque masks. She wanted to walk up and slap every one of them.

She glanced around as if someone might have read her thoughts. Satisfied that her secret was safe, she climbed the steps and fitted her key into the lock on her front door. It was painted bright yellow, the color of hope, and beyond was Julia's orderly cocoon.

The ornate Victorian wall-hung mirror in the hallway showed a tall, slender woman on the wrong side of forty with long blond hair windblown and blue eyes untroubled. Julia Ford, lifestyle columnist for the *Firefly*, a weekly newspaper few outside of Shutter Lake had ever heard of, a paper she'd have dismissed as insignificant before she came here.

She nodded at her reflection, satisfied. Her mask was still in place, but that didn't mean Dana hadn't seen right through her. She was the school principal, a *psychologist*, for Pete's sake. She could spot a lie a mile away, even if it was just a little white one. Why had Julie ever told Dana, of all people, she'd ask for help from her former friend in the FBI, *former* being the operative word?

For reasons too numerous to even think about, Julia would never ask Patrick Richards for help of any kind, professional or otherwise. She could find that girl all by herself, thank you very much.

She kicked off her shoes then padded barefoot across dark oak hardwood floors to her kitchen and the Eastlake sideboard she'd found at a hole-in-the wall store in nearby Grass Valley. Good Stuff, the owner called the store, an apt name for a converted warehouse filled with antiques that would cost twice as much in New Orleans or New York.

Julia filled a mug with hot water from her Keurig then made her favorite drink, green tea chai from a mix she ordered online. No offense to Nolan Ikard down at The Grind. Or to Dana, who was practically addicted to his Macchiato Espressos.

Fading light coming through the stained glass in Julia's kitchen window turned her walls a rainbow of soft pink and gold. She loved that about California - the mild weather and the perpetual sunlight that gave Shutter Lake a golden glow.

Until the glow got tainted by murder. And now a disappearance. A runaway? A kidnapping?

She carried her drink into the sunroom she used as an office – deep wicker chairs with daisy print cushions, glass-topped tables scattered about and littered with magazines on antiques and gardening and music, a small French country desk with a comfortable swivel chair tucked into the corner. Julia flung open the curtain, set her drink on the trivet she kept on her desk and powered up her computer.

"Let's see where you're hiding, Josie Rodriguez."

A photo in the society pages of an earlier issue of the *Firefly* showed an exotic dark-eyed teenager, now seventeen according to Dana. Her uncommon beauty was set off by a lace gown and pearls, compliments, no doubt, of the Windermeres who flanked her. The caption underneath read *Benefactors of Shutter Lake Symphony Orchestra with Exchange Student.*

Josie was named only once in the full page article about Katherine and Quentin Windermere, her host family who not only funded the city's symphony but also its community theater and ballet. The arts community had other benefactors, of course. The town was filled with wealthy families who had distinguished themselves in the fields of science and medicine, mathematics and technology. But none gave so generously as the Windermeres, nor made a point to attend every concert, ballet and play performed in Windermere Center for the Arts. The imposing Grecian-inspired structure had been built entirely with their money in the heart of downtown Shutter Lake.

Julia knew this first hand. She was a great lover of music, a passable singer and a better than average pianist. She never missed an arts event in Shutter Lake and had interviewed the Windermeres many times in the last few years.

She grabbed pen and pad and started writing. *Symphony, Katherine W.*

Her cell phone blared out "Crazy." Her mother's signature ring. Not surprising coming from a Tennessee-born woman who grew up in the town Patsy Cline helped make famous. When Julia was ten her mother had packed them off to Chicago where Rachel proceeded to become the belle of the Windy City.

"Mom? What…"

"It's all over the news about that poor girl's murder. I think you ought to come home where you'll be safe."

Julia's mother never said *hello* when she called. She just barreled into whatever subject she had on her mind, completely abandoning the Southern manners she trotted out with regularity in public. Rachel Maddox Ford Chin was nothing if not the Grand Dame of Chicago society.

Julia pictured her mother, an older and shorter but more elegant version of herself, standing in her expensive penthouse apartment - a modern conglomeration of glass and steel - and gazing at a sweeping view of the Windy City's skyline. Her blond hair would be swept into a French twist and she'd probably be dressed in slacks and one of her ubiquitous silk blouses, tucked in to show off her still-trim waistline. She would *definitely* be biting off her pink lipstick while she twisted the ever-present rope of pearls around her neck.

"Mom, if I were any safer, I'd be dead. This is the first murder in Shutter Lake's history, and even if I wanted to write about crime, there's none to report."

Until now.

"I'm *glad* you're writing about Beethoven and beef stew instead of cat burglars and serial killers. And so is Joe. He thinks you ought to come home, too. I'd just die if anything happened to you out there in the wilds."

"I'm not in the wilds, and nothing's going to happen to me."

Even as Julia said it, a wave of homesickness washed over her. Eating hot dogs in Wrigley Field, made as only Chicago can. Browsing museums with her mom. Sailing on Lake Michigan with Joe and that bossy Lhasa Apso he named Sweetie Pie, which said everything you needed to know about the man who'd been the only real father Julia ever knew.

"That does not make me feel one bit better, Julia. That poor dead girl probably thought she was safe, too."

"Her name is Sylvia. Sylvia Cole."

Was. Past tense.

It hit Julia hard that the very thing she'd run from had finally caught up with her – crime, the more sensational the better for the media. She'd covered that beat for years for the *Chicago World,* the *Tribune's* and the *Sun-Times'* biggest rival. Too many years to think about. Too many memories.

Julia pushed them aside and took a long, fortifying drink of her green tea chai. It had gone cold, but that didn't matter. She wasn't as picky about her drinks as Dana.

"You see?" Her mother let out a sigh that bordered on drama-queen level. "That's just what I'm talking about. That pitiful departed soul was somebody's little girl, just like you're mine. My *only* little girl."

"According to all the black balloons I avoided like the plague on my last birthday, your little girl is over the hill, Mom." Her mother chuckled, as Julia had intended. "Is Joe there?"

"Not yet, but he'll be here in about fifteen minutes. Let me run and get some tea then we'll chat 'til he gets here."

Julia almost let out a dramatic sigh of her own. "I can't. I've got things to do."

"What can be more important than talking to your mother? Maybe Joe can talk some sense into you."

Julia would love to talk to him, if nothing else just to let the lilting sound of his voice conjure up happy memories of a childhood spent tagging along behind him, asking a million questions. He always answered with the patience of Buddha. Her stepfather would press his case for her return, but in a way that was soft-spoken and polite.

A way that reminded her of Chief of Police Griff McCabe. And the entire falling-down house of cards that had once been the nation's perfect city.

"I really have to go, Mom."

Before Rachel could marshal any more arguments, Julia said goodbye and ended the connection. Her computer had gone into rest mode and she brought it back to life.

"Let's see what else you've been up to, Josie."

School events and academic awards in math, science and music. She'd been a star student with an incredibly bright future, which made her disappearance all the more puzzling. The selection process for exchange students was rigorous at the prestigious Shutter Lake School. After winning one of the coveted spots why would a girl making such stellar grades give it up? Especially when school was in session?

Julia continued to scan the articles. Josie had been photographed in more public appearances with the Windemeres. She had the kind of face loved by a camera lens. And she made the philanthropic white-haired couple, a handsome pair, look even better. No wonder the press always aimed a camera at her.

"Pictures never tell the true story." Had the Windermere's been using their exchange students to make them look good? Was their well-documented philanthropy an attempt to hide a dark purpose?

She printed off a good headshot of Josie and made a note to call Katherine Windermere for an interview. Symphony season was in high gear, with a fundraiser planned on the park for Saturday. She had the perfect angle to question the woman.

The Windermeres had been on Julia's radar for some time now, well before Sylvia's death. The parade of foreign exchange students going in and out of their home had put her instincts on high alert. With Josie's disappearance, she could no longer ignore her intuition. She knew how to segue from music to a missing teenager, and she had a knack for getting people to reveal more than they intended.

Julia continued her cyber search and her note taking in the methodical, from-the-ground-up manner that had served her well in her days of investigative journalism. With a jolt she realized she'd missed this. Periodically her former editor emailed or called to lure her back. He wanted her full-time again in Chicago. Lately, he'd said he would settle for freelance in Shutter Lake.

Big stories, though. Not her current life-style pabulum. His words, not hers.

It wasn't until her stomach rumbled that she realized she'd missed supper, whatever that was. Probably soup from a can.

She also noticed that her curtains were still wide open to a sky turned deep velvet. Forbidding. The only light in the room came from her computer screen and the nightlight plugged in behind a glass-top table.

Julia sprang up so fast she almost toppled her chair, a nearly impossible feat considering it was on a swivel base. Her heart raced as she flew around her house closing curtains against the darkness, checking locks on windows and doors against anything evil that lurked in the shadows…and most of all, making certain all her nightlights were burning.

Julia felt the almost-forgotten beginnings of a panic attack coming on.

She said a word she used to see on the walls of bathrooms before she moved to a town that kept everything pristine, including public toilets. Then she felt a foolish stab of guilt, as if she'd betrayed her mother. How many times had Rachel, the consummate Southern belle, reminded her that a woman who made her living stringing words together ought to have a vocabulary that would express her dismay without resorting to the mouth of a common gutter snipe.

She said it again on general principles, but also because the sound of her own voice stilled her panic. She was in the here and now, not back in the nightmare that had sent her running so hard and fast it took the edge of a continent and the Pacific Ocean to stop her. Though, practically speaking, she wasn't close enough to see the ocean without a considerable drive.

"Not today, you don't." She rubbed her forehead then took a deep breath, consciously relaxed her clenched jaw and waited.

Nothing. Good.

She made a rude gesture though nobody could possibly see, not with those blackout curtains on every window. Then she marched into her kitchen and opened a can of tomato soup. Plain. No frills. She loved cooking and she particularly loved experimenting, but tonight she was in no mood to add butter and real cream. Or maybe cream cheese with a touch of dill.

Julia ate her soup standing up, still tense, ever vigilant, turning her head toward every sound. The high-pitched voices of the nine-year-old twin boys next door, arguing with their mother about coming inside to eat. The metallic clang of a metal garbage can across her back fence. The sound of an engine, slowing as it entered the neighborhood and then stopped.

So close. Next door?

Her adrenaline surged as she crept toward the front of her house. The sound outside her door tipped her closer toward the edge of panic. Footsteps, definitely. Her friends *never* showed up without calling first. They knew better.

Had her past finally caught up with her? Was another dark horror waiting just beyond her door, taunting her that *this time* there would be no escape?

Don't Miss

If you enjoyed *so many secrets*, please consider leaving a review so other reader's can find it, too.

Read Dana's short read: the story of the incident that forever changed her life, *her deepest fear*. Available at Amazon.

The BREAKDOWN Novels
the dead girl by Debra Webb
so many secrets by Vicki Hinze
all the lies by Peggy Webb
what she knew by Regan Black

The BREAKDOWN Short Reads

no looking back by Debra Webb
her deepest fear by Vicki Hinze
just one look by Peggy Webb
trust no one by Regan Black

About the Author

Vicki Hinze is a *USA Today* bestselling author who has written nearly forty books, fiction and nonfiction, and hundreds of articles, published in as many as 63 countries. She's won a wide array of awards, including novels of the year in multiple genres. All of her novels, general market (secular) or inspirational, include suspense, mystery and romance. The focus determines genre. Her works have been classified in nearly every genre except horror, with the majority being suspense, thriller, mystery and romance.

As well as a Vice President for International Thriller Writers, Vicki has served as a consultant to the Board of Directors for Romance Writers of America and several other notable organizations. She is the former host of radio talk show, *Everyday Woman*, and a current columnist for Social In, a global network.

Vicki was the first RWA PRO Mentor of the Year, and the recipient of the National Service Award. She's also recognized as an author and an educator by *Who's Who in the World*.

For early access to new releases and more, subscribe to the monthly newsletter at http://mad.ly/signups/82943/join

Also by Vicki Hinze

Breakdown
so many secrets | her deepest fear (Short Read)

Down and Dead, Inc.
Down and Dead in Dixie | Down and Dead in Even
Down and Dead in Dallas

Shadow Watchers
(Crossroads Crisis Center related)
The Marked Star | The Marked Bride
Wed to Death: Short Read

Crossroads Crisis Center
Forget Me Not | Deadly Ties
Not This Time

The Reunited Hearts Collection
Her Perfect Life | Mind Reader
Duplicity

Lost, Inc.
Survive the Night | Christmas Countdown
Torn Loyalties

War Games
Body Double | Double Vision | Double Dare

Smokescreen: Total Recall (Double Recall) | Kill Zone

The Lady Duo
Lady Liberty | Lady Justice

Military
Shades of Gray | Duplicity | Acts of Honor
All Due Respect

Seascape
Beyond the Misty Shore | Upon a Mystic Tide
Beside a Dreamswept Sea

For a complete listing of all Vicki's books, visit:
vickihinze.com/books

Made in the USA
San Bernardino, CA
02 August 2019